DRUNK ON YOU

A BOURBON BOYS STORY

TERI ANNE STANLEY

Entangled Publishing, LLC
2614 South Timberline Road
Suite 109
Fort Collins, CO 80525
Visit our website at www.entangledpublishing.com.

Lovestruck is an imprint of Entangled Publishing, LLC.

Edited by Robin Haseltine
Cover design by Heather Howland
Cover art by iStock

Manufactured in the United States of America

First Edition July 2015

For everyone who didn't come home. And everyone who did.

Chapter One

Eight years ago

Ladies' room, Blue Grass Airport, Lexington, Kentucky

"Allie McGrath, I'm not going to stand here holding all this stuff while you brush your teeth again," Eve said. "I can't believe you brought your toothbrush to the airport. That's just…nasty. Airport bathrooms are nasty. Get some gum. I'll even pay for it."

Allie ignored her older sister and dug in her purse for dental floss. She'd gone to too much trouble to get ready for this homecoming to ruin it all by greeting her marine with poor dental hygiene.

Eve rolled her eyes and followed Allie into the restroom, lugging the red, white, and blue balloons and the giant Welcome Home, Justin poster that was covered with kisses Allie had made with her own lips and red lipstick.

As Allie brushed and flossed for the third time that day, she checked her appearance in the mirror. "Do you think this shirt highlights my pudge?" She pinched her waist.

"You don't have any pudge. You've Pilates'ed yourself into oblivion. I can't believe you've gone to this much trouble for someone you've known your whole life."

Allie stared at Eve in the mirror. "You have to ask me this?"

"He and David spent a whole spring break in our family room one year learning to make arm farts." And then he'd spent his entire allowance on Allie's extra unsold Girl Scout cookies. Even the furniture-polish-flavored ones that no one liked.

"But now it's different. He's more than just our brother's best friend," Allie protested.

She turned sideways. The top *was* a little clingy around the waist, but it *did* make her boobs look bigger. Of course, Victoria's Secret helped with that, too. She sucked in her stomach. "I should have worn a skirt. These pants aren't nice enough."

"A skirt would have been too much. The chances that Justin even bothered to put on clean camouflage for the plane ride are pretty slim."

Allie regarded Eve. She didn't get it. Her sister was being pretty supportive, though, considering she thought Allie was making a big mistake in coming here at all. But Allie knew what she was doing. Justin would be *so* glad to see her…she was, after all, "his girl."

He'd said so, in his last email:

Thanks for the goodies. The guys think I'm the shit with a sweet young thing sending me stuff, along with those notes. They're all jealous.

Be my girl and don't stop! Can't wait to see you when I get home next month.

Allie knew it was childish, but she'd printed that email and taped it into the journal she'd used for the last half of senior year at Crockett County High.

"Come on, Al, it's time to go."

Her stomach dropped. She'd been so focused on this moment for so long, now that it was finally here, she thought she might throw up from nerves. Fortunately, she had a toothbrush with her if that happened...

"Just a minute. I've got to pee." She shut herself into a stall and stood there for a second, breathing deeply.

A toilet flushed, and another stall opened. Someone said, "Hi, Eve. What are you doing here?"

"Waiting for my sister."

"Who are you—?" There was a pause. "Oh, isn't that a nice poster. Justin Morgan, huh?"

Who was that? The voice was familiar, but Allie couldn't place it.

"Who are *you* meeting?" Eve sounded wary, a little chilly even.

"Oh, an old friend," the person answered. Water ran, and then the paper towel dispenser ground, drowning out whatever Eve said in response.

"Okay, well, y'all have fun," said the voice.

Allie came out of the stall and looked around. "Who was that?" she asked, washing her own hands.

"Al, maybe we should head home and wait for Justin there. You know he'll come over as soon as his mom and dad let him."

"What's wrong with you?" Allie took the balloons and the sign.

Eve opened her mouth, but shut it again.

Allie walked out of the bathroom. "Oh, heck! We're gonna be late!" She hurried through the baggage claim area to the security zone, waiting for the love of her life to come striding through the concourse. She was *so* ready to greet him. She'd even been to the clinic and gotten on the pill, because she planned to lose her virginity to Justin just as soon as she got him alone.

There was a crowd of people ahead of Allie watching for loved ones to come through the gate, so she hung back. That would give her more room for a running start when he finally appeared.

A rustle went through the crowd, and she stood on tiptoe to see over the heads in front of her. An Amazonian blonde, in particular, was wrecking her view.

A few people came through the gate, and then a whole crowd. Allie couldn't see anything. She pushed her way forward, through the throng, and there he was.

Justin Morgan. Her marine, all six feet two, two hundred pounds of gorgeous USMC hotness. His blue eyes pierced the crowd, searching, the ever-present half smile on his face, waiting to bloom into the full-fledged shit-eating grin that Allie had loved forever.

She froze in place watching him approach. He was close now. Her face was hot. This was really happening.

"Hey, there's my girl!" His voice rang out, deep and true.

He stopped about six feet away, those teeth as straight and white as ever. God, Allie loved him.

The searing pain of her shattered heart kept her from puking when he swept the statuesque blonde into his arms and thrust his tongue down her throat.

Chapter Two

"I've got it, Grandma," Justin promised, hoisting the ancient fur coat from where she'd dropped it in the valet parking lane before the furry abomination was mistaken for roadkill.

"You make sure you get a ticket from that coat check girl. She screws it up otherwise." Grandma shook her finger. "We always wind up standing an extra half hour while she looks for my wrap."

"That's because she wants to get in my pants," Grandpa said, wiggling his eyebrows.

"It's a wonder I've stayed married to you long enough to have this ridiculous anniversary party." Grandma smacked Gramps on the shoulder, but they held hands as they made their way toward the ballroom of the Crockett County Country Club.

Justin sighed and turned toward the cloakroom. The generous shot of bourbon he drank before leaving home hadn't been quite enough.

He'd spent part of his youth here at "the club"—life-guarding at the pool and caddying at the golf course—because even though they might be an old bourbon family, their dad was determined that his boys would learn to work for their money. He'd also brought his prom date to dinner here and learned to play tennis and to schmooze with the good old boys—but now he felt like an alien from planet Armageddon among these civilians with their happy, normal lives.

He was just here for this anniversary party and to say hello to his family—and the McGraths—whom he'd been avoiding since Dave died. Not that it was hard to be too busy to call from a war zone, but it was rude, and he'd promised Dave...

Yeah, he'd promised Dave he'd look in on his sisters, especially Allie. Little redheaded Allie with the funny cards and packages. That had dried up a few years ago, even before Dave died, but she must have discovered boys and forgotten about his crusty old soul. Just as well. Someone as sweet and innocent as Allie didn't need to be worrying about him and his toxic world. He went to war so people like her didn't have to live through it. Except he didn't do that anymore, did he? He was a civilian now.

Maybe he needed, as his brother, Brandon, had suggested, to go out and meet a girl and have a good time. He was going to be in town for only a few days, and he wasn't sure he could dig out the Justin Morgan charm he'd once been infamous for. But a distraction would be nice...for a while.

The half door stood open. The four hundred-year-old coat check woman wasn't at her post, so Justin walked into the dim room to stash Grandma's coat. He stepped around the end of the coatrack and plowed crotch-first into the finest backside he'd encountered, ass-up, in quite some time—possibly ever.

"Yeep!" The voice attached to the perfect ass squealed and the rest of the body straightened and turned to face him.

Damn.

"Excuse me. Er, didn't see you there." Justin reached out to steady the woman as she wobbled on high heels. She was a blonde, he could see that much, but her features were backlit by the setting sun shining through the window. Her perfume seemed almost familiar. He breathed deeply of… home and…peace.

She slid the coat hanger she held onto the rack.

He wondered what color her eyes were. And if those glossy lips tasted as juicy as they looked. Shaking it off, he released his hold on her smooth arm and backed up a step, admiring the silky red dress she wore. Not tight or revealing, but definitely clingy. Subtle, yet…obvious.

"Ah…" She shook her head and asked, "Do you need help with your fine mink coat, sir?"

He held up Grandma's ridiculous fur. It was heavy enough for an Eskimo, even though it was late spring. "You don't look like the coat check lady I remember."

"Really? People tell me I'm the spitting image of her."

"Interesting," Justin said. "I didn't know there was anyone here old enough to have been around during the Civil War, who'd have known her in her youth."

The woman giggled, and Justin realized he was actually

flirting. And enjoying himself. He'd drunk just enough to wonder... Would it be tacky to hit on the coat check girl? She seemed familiar. Maybe they'd worked together at the pool back in their younger days?

"You're a flatterer, aren't you? You know she was born during the Renaissance."

Those lips curled, making Justin want to lean forward and taste them. Damn. *Okay, Brandon, you win. I'll ask her out.*

"Well, it's clear you haven't been around nearly that long. As a matter of fact, I was just thinking that maybe you'd sneak away from here after a while and dance with me."

"Hmm... Are we talking the Macarena, or the Electric Slide?"

"I was thinking something slower and closer."

"Ah. Well, then. I guess I'll have to think about that."

"Well, don't think too long." He wasn't sure how long he'd be able to stand it here among the normal people. He summoned a chuckle then and held out his hand. "I'm Justin Morgan. And you are...?"

"Seriously?" She didn't take his hand, but put hers on her hips.

"Yeah? Come on, babe, give me a shot." He dusted off his trademarked crooked smile. "It's not my best pickup line, but you get the idea, right?"

She nodded. "Yeah, unfortunately, I do." She handed him the hanger she'd just put away as she brushed past. "Get your grandma a ticket, Justin, otherwise she'll bitch about the coat check lady flirting with Gramps."

The dust left Justin's brain with an artillery blast as he realized whom he was trying to pick up in the coatroom. He stuck his head through the door in time to see her walk down the hall. Holy shit. "Hey, Allie. When did you go blond?"

• • •

"Come on, Allie, you're going to have to go out there and see him sooner or later," Eve said.

Allie wrinkled her brow in her best, "What are you talking about?" expression, running a finger under her eye to remove a mascara smudge. She tugged at her new blond highlights. Maybe she'd gone too far? Nah, she was still definitely ginger. To everyone but certain buttface jerkheads.

It was clear that Eve wasn't buying what she was trying to sell, but the most awesome sister ever wasn't going to call her on her bullshit—yet.

"You know Justin's out there."

"Really? I'd forgotten he was back in town."

Eve rolled her eyes.

Okay, maybe that was taking it a little too far. Eve *had* seen Allie slam into the bathroom, and Allie had heard Eve say, "Hi, Justin," right before she followed her in.

She'd managed to live a well-rounded, boyfriend-filled life without being ego-bashed by Justin Morgan for the past seven years, ten months, three days, and fourteen hours—give or take—apparently biding her time until she could make a fool of herself. Again.

"What happened when you saw him?" Eve pressed.

Allie sighed, giving in. "He flirted with me in the coatroom when I was hanging up our stuff."

"Really?" Eve's big dark eyes widened, her perfect red lips forming an O.

"And I bought it. It was like he waved his magic wang, and I totally forgot how I'm not a gullible teenager anymore. Right up until I realized that he had no idea who I was."

"Oh." Now Eve had on her best indignant-sister face. If she weren't so sincere, Allie would hate her for always having the right sympathetic emotion to toss out there when needed. Allie shrugged.

"Come on, we've got to go out there sometime. Might as well get it over with," Eve coaxed.

Allie's laugh sounded forced, even to her own ears— and her sister was a million and seven times more perceptive than anyone else Allie knew. But she persisted. "It's fine. God, I can't believe you think I'm still twisted up over that... that...airport thing."

"You did cry for three weeks straight, eat your weight— and mine—in Cherry Garcia ice cream, and play *Patsy Cline's Greatest Hits* until the CD melted. I think we both know you were crushed when he came home to Merilee."

It hadn't helped when Allie realized that it had been Merilee—Justin's high school sweetheart and psycho bitch from hell—to whom Eve had been speaking in the restroom that day, and when the beyotch finished trying to swallow Justin's tongue, she'd turned and winked at Allie.

"But then I turned up the Miranda Lambert and moved on." Or at least, learned to pretend Justin's non-betrayal— because he'd never considered her his girl at all—hadn't meant anything. But the truth was, she had been devastated. And embarrassed. And mortified. And heartbroken.

Gah! *Enough.* It totally didn't matter that Justin Morgan had broken her heart eight long years ago. That was water under the bridge. She was fine now. She'd had boyfriends—

lots of boyfriends—and she was way past being the naive teenager who'd taken the casual words of a far-off, lonely soldier to heart.

Allie couldn't care less that Justin Morgan was in the same state, same county—or even the same room—as her because her give-a-damn had broken a long time ago.

"Let's go sample the moonshine."

Eve laughed and opened the door for Allie to lead the way to the ballroom. "Don't let Mother hear you compare Blue Mountain bourbon to moonshine. She'll make you sleep in the rickhouse."

"If she'd get her head out of the seventies, she might appreciate what I'm trying to tell her about Blue Mountain and white dog."

"Not tonight, Allie, please?"

"Fine." But she'd find a way to get her baby whiskey to market with or without the support of Blue Mountain.

"I think Justin's dad's about to make his toast," Eve said, pulling Allie toward their table near the dance floor. Lorena pursed her lips when her daughters approached. As they took their seats and apologized to their mother for their tardiness, Justin's father, the current CEO of Blue Mountain Bourbon , stood and tapped the microphone.

Damn. She'd known this was coming, and she appreciated it—her whole family did—but... Allie took a deep breath and let it out slowly, keeping her eyes wide so that any tears might pool in her lower lids but not spill.

"Ladies and gentlemen, I'd like to thank you all for being here tonight to celebrate the love my parents have for each other. We've already toasted their anniversary, and we're going to get to the dancing here in just a minute, but

I'd like to take a minute to honor another family member who isn't with us tonight."

The crowd, seated at banquet tables around the room, quieted. They knew what was coming, too.

From the corner of her eye, Allie saw Justin make his way to the back of the room, toward the bar. She couldn't have missed him, even though she might have pretended to try. She turned to look at him fully. He was, impossibly, more handsome than he'd ever been. Still tall, still muscular, light brown hair a little longer than he'd worn it before. Tonight, his broad shoulders seemed more rigid than straight. Even through the mud-colored glasses of her own hurt feelings, she recognized that his carefree flirting in the coatroom hadn't been the natural reflex she remembered. War had changed him. As she stared, he looked straight at her.

She smiled, saucily. Or at least, that's what she tried for.

He held her eyes for a long moment, and though she knew he'd always been a player, that he didn't really see her any differently from any other woman he'd ever known, her blood heated when he carried that gaze to body parts her dress was supposed to keep hidden.

Then he gave the briefest of nods and turned away.

His father continued, "Ten years ago, my son Brandon graduated from Crockett County High School. He was followed a year later by his brother, Justin, and their best friend, David McGrath. As you know, Brandon went to UK and then came home to take his place at Blue Mountain, right at a time we needed him most."

Lorena stiffened at the reminder of how Eve and Allie's dad had died and left the BMB's finances in precarious shape.

But Clyde had never blamed Lorena for what was in the past, the business was recovering, and he went on with his speech. "Justin and David took another path."

Everyone turned to look at Justin, who, shoulders tense, kept his gaze fixed on the parquet floor, waiting for his drink.

"The Morgans and McGraths have a long tradition, of not only making the finest bourbon in Kentucky, but of serving our country with honor. Our boys always came home, usually with a chest full of medals and a wealth of stories."

Allie gave up, relaxed her face, and accepted the Kleenex that Eve handed to her. She resisted the urge to turn and see if Justin was still there or if he'd escaped. Waiters were making their way through the room, putting small red, white, and blue gift bags on every table.

"Two years ago, however, we learned that United States Marine Corps Sergeant David Sean McGrath had been killed in Afghanistan."

Next to her, Eve sniffled. Allie reached out a hand, which her sister took. A gentle touch sent a warm shiver through her. She jerked to see Justin brush past. Had that been on purpose? He didn't look back at her as he sat down two tables away.

"So in honor of the life of Sergeant Dave McGrath, I'd like to introduce our newest bourbon, Dangerous Dave's 8-Ball, which is from the last batch David was home to distill, from a small pot still that he and Justin set up and ran while they were both here on leave. We're incredibly grateful to have Justin home to keep the brand alive, and look forward to his future contributions to Blue Mountain Bourbon."

Allie turned her head in time to see Justin straighten, reaching for the bag at the table next to him. He pulled out the half-pint bottle that all the guests would take home, a miniature of the fifth that his father held up at the front of the room.

"So without further ado, here's to you, Sergeant McGrath!" Clyde held up his glass, and everyone else in the room did the same.

Except Justin. Allie watched as Justin unscrewed the top of the little bottle and poured half of it straight down his throat.

Then he lowered the bottle, watching Allie, and put the lid back on. She felt the heat in her belly spreading through her limbs, as though she'd downed her own shot. He didn't look away until Clara Horvath stopped next to his chair and groped his arm, clearly admiring his impressive muscles. He grinned at the over-perfumed old lady and opened up a can of the famous Morgan family charm, complete with that grin. He said something that Allie couldn't hear, but it made the old woman purse her lips, then smile and smack him on the shoulder.

As Allie's mother claimed her attention, she thought she saw Justin look over at her again.

Allie poured her own generous slug of Dangerous Dave into a glass before she drank it.

• • •

"You could just ask her to dance," Brandon said, dropping into a chair at the big round table.

Justin leaned back and drained his third—or maybe it was his fourth, it didn't really matter, it wouldn't be his last— shot of Blue Mountain bourbon of the night. Not counting the two or three ounces of 8-Ball he'd chugged. He watched the "her" in question—or rather, he watched her hips—doing some sort of intricate sway and wiggle as she danced with his second cousin's boyfriend's four-year-old. "I don't think so," he finally said.

He was considering it, an hour ago, before he realized she was Dave's little sister. Allie Fucking McGrath? No way.

"What's the problem?" Brandon asked. "It's just Allie. She doesn't bite."

The legs of his chair hit the ground with a thud. "Oh, hell no."

"Why not? She's single."

"She's...*hot*."

Brandon looked at Justin like he'd sprouted an extra pair of eyes. "Why is that a problem? You knew this, right?"

"I never... I mean, I saw pictures on Facebook a few years ago, but after Dave died, I just didn't..." He couldn't bear to see what was going on at home. So he never looked. He figured he'd see sorrow and accusation staring back at him.

But he couldn't ignore her anymore, because he'd made a promise. He was home now, so he had to man up and follow through.

They ignore her, treat her like she's a little kid, Dave had said. *Make sure she's gonna be okay.*

From where Justin was sitting, she was more than okay. And she certainly wasn't the little kid he remembered. Little Allie McGrath had followed Dave and him around, complaining that all Eve wanted to do was play Barbies. Allie wanted in on their football, video, or God help him, war games. Or she needed help with her latest scheme to earn a million dollars. He'd somehow always gotten suckered into playing along with those—but who wouldn't have agreed to help hold a car wash for horses? It's not like anyone ever showed up to get their horse washed, and he'd get to sit in a lawn chair and avoid yard work while he "helped" Allie.

When the hell had she grown up? She'd been sweet when she was in high school, writing to him and sending him packages. But then she must have gotten interested in some boy here in Crockett County, because the mail dried up. By then, the war had taken all of his attention and energy. And then it had taken his soul.

And now, here he was. Nothing to offer but his own nightmares, so maybe if he fulfilled his promise to Dave... maybe he could get some sleep. He hoped she needed something easy...wallpaper, paint, hell—he'd even donate a kidney. As long as he could do it and get the hell out of Crockett County before he lost his shit.

But there she was, just a few feet away on the dance floor, distracting him from the ever-present rumble of military vehicles and explosions that lived behind his eyes.

Damn. Curves dipping, swaying—and occasionally jiggling—setting a kid down, laughing when he kissed her cheek and ran back to his mom.

He nodded to another family friend, here to drink a toast or three for Gran and Grandpa Morgan's anniversary. What could have been a pleasant evening, with flowing booze and a decent band, had been wrecked with the kick in the balls that was the introduction of Dave's memorial bourbon brand—and gee, Dad, thanks for adding on the little dig about how he was expected to stick around and work at the fucking miserable booze factory.

There wasn't a chance in hell that he'd stay in Crockett County long enough to help bottle a case of bourbon, much less run an entire division, which was what his father wanted—had wanted for him since he was old enough to walk. Nope, he was out of here and on the next flight to smoke-jumper school as soon as the rest of the family left for Grandma and Gramps's anniversary cruise.

Until the band started playing Macklemore's "Can't Hold Us," and Allie danced. Then the previously sedate evening went from party to par-tay, and Justin's night got a lot more complicated. How the hell was he supposed to look out for this girl? She was supposed to still be an awkward teenager. Not this…this poster girl for dirty thoughts. He had to get out of town. Sooner rather than later. He ordered another drink from a passing waiter, but it didn't cool him off or in any other way stop him from wanting to pick Allie up and drag her out of the reception hall to see if she wore a thong under that dress, as he suspected. There was no panty line at the leg, but maybe something at her waist… He groaned when she turned toward him, and he was able to confirm that whatever she had on the bottom, she couldn't possibly be wearing a bra.

"Where's your girlfriend?" Justin asked Brandon, trying to divert his attention elsewhere.

"Ah, that's over," Brandon said, pulling his phone out and tapping the screen in an obvious attempt to close the subject.

"Whoa, what happened? I thought you were hot and heavy with…um…Cheryl?"

"Charlene. And I thought we were, too. But apparently my idea of hot and heavy and hers don't mesh. It seems I'm boring."

Justin looked at his older brother. They shared the same parents, the same basic genes, but where Justin was the meathead, muscle-bound oaf, Brandon was the long, lean brainiac. From his medium-short brown hair to his tidy but not obsessively neat attire, Brandon was…pretty average.

"Buddy," Justin finally said, "you're not boring, you just haven't met the perfect woman yet."

"You mean the perfectly dull girl?" Brandon gestured at Allie. "I'm not seeing someone like Allie for me. Now, you, on the other hand—you could handle all that energy."

"Not in a million years." Although it might just happen in his fantasies, if he wasn't careful.

A couple stopped by his chair to shake his hand and welcome him home. He managed to "Hey-how-ya-doin'-good-ta-see-ya" them without getting stuck hearing about the man's own Semper Fi memories.

Then Grandpa attempted something that might have been a geriatric version of twerking and backed into Allie, whose four-inch heels went out from under her. Her legs flew into the air, and she landed on her luscious backside, sprawled in front of Justin.

Laughing, she looked up. Her green eyes sparkled in the light from the disco ball, wild strawberry-blond hair winning the battle against whatever hairdo thing she'd used to hold it all twisted up on her head. She was, indeed, wearing a thong. A red one. "Um, oops." She tugged her skirt down, but not quite far enough.

Justin's bourbon-marinated reflexes were a little slow, but he still beat Brandon to the punch and helped Allie to her feet. He ignored his brother's smirk.

And Allie's smile. He understood that it had been too sad at Blue Mountain for too long. But he had no business being on the receiving end of that sweet, hot gaze.

Once she was steady on her feet, he grabbed his suit jacket from the back of his chair and escaped through a nearby door onto the patio.

The cool April night allowed his presence. Not welcoming, but not a cold tolerance, either. Justin stared out over the gently rolling hills of the golf course to the McMansions beyond, at warm, lighted windows protecting the families inside from weather and reality. Through the picture window of the nearest house, lights of a giant flat screen TV flickered. From where he stood, it looked like a video game with a lot of explosions was in progress.

He thought of his brothers-in-arms who would be freezing their asses off somewhere on patrol, if it was night in Afghanistan—or sweating their balls off if it wasn't—so those kids could play *World of Warcraft* on leather couches while their Botoxed, siliconed soccer moms fed them healthy snacks and Ritalin.

He thought of Dave, who wasn't sweating or freezing anywhere anymore.

The door behind Justin opened, letting out a wedge of light chased with music and conversation. He didn't turn to see who it was, but a faint herbal scent preceded the appearance of Allie a few feet away. Think of the devil, and his sister appears.

The clip of her footsteps slowed, as though she was uncertain about the wisdom of speaking to him. He didn't blame her.

Warmth seeped through his suit coat and shirtsleeve as

she neared. "Are you okay?" She entered his field of view, and the visions of Afghanistan faded from his memory.

She wasn't wearing anything over that curve-hugging dress, and she shivered a little, making him want to put an arm around her shoulder. Just to keep her warm.

"Sure, Sneezy, just thinking about finding a cigar." He used the nickname they'd saddled Allegra with when she was a kid on purpose, to remind himself that this was his dead best friend's baby sister and not his own personal siren.

Her vaguely husky laugh wound through his buzz, stirring his blood. "You'll have to sneak farther than the patio for a smoke. The Ladies Who Lunch have forbidden tobacco products within a hundred yards of the clubhouse."

"You're kidding. Half their membership dues have been paid by tobacco money."

Allie shrugged, a move that drew his eye to her cleavage. He couldn't help himself—he was conditioned to pay attention to danger, and those breasts were a hazard to his sanity.

She caught his glance and blushed as she tugged self-consciously at the neckline.

"Are you okay after that fall inside?" he asked. To have something to do besides ogle her, he pulled a flask from his jacket pocket.

"More or less." She took the flask from his hand and tipped it to soft pink lips. Her nipples would be the same color, he realized. She poured a healthy shot of bourbon down her throat and swallowed without a grimace.

Atta girl.

"That toast your dad made was nice," she said.

"Yeah."

"David would have thought it was wack, but I bet he

would have liked the name of the bourbon."

"Yeah." He should say something more, but his tongue felt thick. The subject of Dave paralyzed his vocal cords.

"Brandon said you're leaving in a few days to start training as a smoke jumper or something out West?"

"Yep." That was a better subject. Almost. "One of my buddies has a cousin who contracts with the Forest Service."

One perfect eyebrow rose. "It's gonna be hard to be the brand manager for Dangerous Dave's if you're putting out forest fires, isn't it?"

He took the flask back and capped it, sliding it into his jacket. "My dad's making assumptions I'm going to work here. I didn't agree to that." Which was an understatement, but that was a battle for another day.

She put her hands on her hips. "No one bothered to ask *me* if I was interested in the job, but I guess that's 'cause they were saving it for you."

"Maybe they will now." Maybe he could make that happen for her, get her the job, and then his "look out for Allie" promise would be fulfilled. "Anyway, I have the job out West all lined up, so…"

"Why?" Her sweet nose wrinkled in confusion. "Why would you get out of one war just to go back into another crazy, dangerous job?"

He thought about telling her the truth. That it was all he was good at. That everything here — all this quiet comfort and normality — would strangle him if he stayed. Or he would explode all over and tarnish it. Instead, he said, "Eh, I guess I've developed a taste for adrenaline. Big money, big adventure…" Her soft green eyes told him she wasn't buying it.

They were both quiet then, glances meeting and then caroming away. Awkwardness began to settle through the night air. Justin shuffled his foot, and a loose pebble rolled down the steps. He cleared his throat, wanting to ask what she needed, what he had to do to fulfill his promise to Dave to look out for her. The strains of some old Barry Manilow song drifted from the dance floor. Instead of turning to go back inside, she stepped closer and twined long, slender arms around his neck.

Chapter Three

Allie wasn't sure what had made her follow Justin outside. Testing herself, she supposed. The extra shot of bourbon after his father's toast might have something to do with her compulsion to make a fool of herself, too. And the slug from the flask was definitely responsible for her current position, pressed against the hard planes of his chest.

His hands came up to curve around her waist.

This was crazy. But… "I believe you invited me to dance."

"Probably not a good idea," he murmured, as he pulled her closer and slid his hands farther over her hips, up her back. He didn't sway to the music, but his body was a solid column of heat, and somehow their feet moved them in a slow circle.

The sound of the party inside was faint against the sound of her own sigh. She was slow dancing with Justin Morgan. His shoulders were hard curves beneath her hands, shifting slightly as he moved. "I should have recognized you earlier," he said.

"Would that have been good or bad?" Did she really want to know? Did he see past the dorky teenager she'd been to the hopefully more sophisticated woman she wanted the world to see?

"I don't know, babe." His low chuckle sent a thrill through her. "You're probably safer if I remember you're off-limits."

"Why am I off-limits?"

Her heel caught in a space between two stones, but she thought she heard him say something about "difficult promises" while she wobbled and tipped forward, her body pressing more fully against his and her face tipping up. "Whoa!" She was caught by his gaze, direct and deep.

His eyes reflected the midnight sky, and something else…desire. But was it just a mirror of her own want? *Off-limits,* he'd said…

They weren't turning to the music anymore. Standing still, breath foggy in the dark, bodies aligned, his lips were close. Too close. She shifted, and felt—oh God—his erection, pressing against her belly.

And he was still looking at her.

Her lips parted, tongue darting out to touch her suddenly hypersensitive lower lip. His eyes telegraphed his intent before he bent his head toward her, brushing his lips against hers, lighting a fire in the cold spring night. A small kiss, barely a touch, but she felt it all the way to her core—not just between her legs, but somewhere farther inside, deeper, somewhere not on any anatomy chart.

She gasped as he took the kiss deeper, his lips coaxing hers apart, his tongue sliding in against her own. He tasted of Blue Mountain bourbon, heat, and need.

Allie felt a wall at her back; somehow they'd maneuvered themselves close to the building. Rough brick caught at her skirt when he pulled at the silky fabric, sliding his thigh between hers.

Moaning, she leaned into his leg, the firm muscle only increasing her need to press against him. The ache rose, fast and high, and her legs began to tremble, to tighten.

She reached between them and ran her hand over the front of his pants, feeling him hard under her stroking fingers. He groaned and thrust into her hand. She wanted to reach for his belt buckle to release all that power, but there was a roomful of family just a few feet away. If they took the time to find somewhere more private, this moment would end—this moment that had been a lifetime in the making.

He whispered something against her skin and she clutched him tighter.

"Oh my God, Justin, I'm going to— I'm about to—"

"You're so fucking hot. *Jesus.*" His kiss traveled away from her mouth, over her jaw to her neck, muttering, "That's my girl, ride my leg."

The words hit Allie like a burning glass of rotgut, sending remembered shame and humiliation coursing through her veins. She'd misconstrued those words—"my girl"—once before, and then heard them directed toward someone else.

"No!" She pushed him away.

"What the hell?" Confusion was quickly replaced by horror. "Oh, fuck. I'm sorry. That was *so* out of line. I can't believe I—we—"

She held up a palm to forestall any more discussion.

He ran a hand down his face, then rubbed the back of his

neck, staring at the ground. He didn't look at her, panting.

Pulling at her clothes, she straightened her skirt and tucked a few bits of hair behind her ear. There was no way she was going back into the party like this. A stairway led to a lower-level terrace and the parking lot beyond that. She was too tipsy to drive home, but one of the valets would call her a cab. She just needed to get away right now.

"I've got to go," she said, starting for the stairs.

"Wait. Babe, I'm sorry."

She stopped and looked at him for a moment.

"I just got carried away—it's been so long since—and I've had a lot to drink, so—"

"Yeah, Justin, that's not helping. Go back to the party." She reached the top step and her damned heel caught again, pitching her forward. Just before she toppled over the top step, Justin caught her arm, pulling her back. She regained her footing, but he began to fall forward.

He twisted partially around in midair, but not far enough. His right shoulder slammed against the railing before he bounced headfirst toward the landing below.

• • •

It was surreal—this was completely different from Afghanistan. There was no gunfire, no screams of pain from burned marines, no fucking dust—not a speck. The ambulance was clean and white and everyone called him "sir." But that patch—MEDIC—and those gloves—those blue plastic gloves. Justin was afraid to look at the empty cot on the other side of the aisle, afraid to see Dave's bloodied remains still beneath a white sheet.

Through a haze of pain, Justin saw his mother hike her fancy dress up to her knees and clamber into the back of the ambulance. He tried to smile at her, but was afraid he'd only produced a grimace. She didn't smile back, but sat down in the seat indicated by the EMT and took the hand that didn't have an IV needle embedded in it.

His leg throbbed—okay, sent daggers of excruciating pain through him—steadily, and there was some concern about a head injury, he thought someone said. It was more likely that his confusion and slurred speech were a side effect of booze, but he wasn't going to beg for pain relief, knowing that might lead him to do something stupid. Like call out to Allie.

Before the doors shut, Justin noticed her standing a few feet away. She was pale and trembling, lips pressed together as she stared at him. He forced his lips into something closer to a real smile for her, because the sight of her furrowed brow—over him—did something to his insides that he couldn't bear to examine. A combination of shame at his own behavior and a desire to touch her again—and to go further next time.

Brandon appeared behind her, raising his chin in Justin's direction, indicating that he'd take care of her. Of course he would; Brandon was the big brother. The responsible one. But as the ambulance ground into gear and the siren began to wail, Justin wondered what vibe he'd given off that made his brother think he needed to take care of Allie for him. But that's what Brandon did. Took care of the things everyone else couldn't, wouldn't, or just plain didn't do.

As soon as they were under way, Justin's mother pulled her hand from his and smacked him on the arm. "What were you thinking?"

Oh, shit. Had his mother seen him molesting Allie on the patio? He'd thought they'd been in the shadows before he kissed her, but—

"I can't believe you drank so much. I hope you have a hangover that hurts more than your leg."

Oh. Well. Overindulgence was something he was well acquainted with. "Sorry, Mom."

"Yeah. Well..." She started to cry.

The EMT handed her a tissue and went back to writing something on a clipboard. Crying mothers were probably just part of a day's work for him.

"Ah, hell, Mom. Don't cry. I'm sorry. I just...I didn't eat any lunch today, and—"

She smacked him again. "Don't bullshit me. I saw how much you drank. I just wish...I wish you would talk to me instead of trying to self-anesthetize. Or, if you can't talk to me, because I just don't 'get it,' talk to your dad. Or your brother. Or one of those veterans support groups."

Oh, fuck. This wasn't about getting drunk at Grandma and Grandpa's anniversary party. And there was nothing he was going to say that would satisfy her belief in the power of the all-knowing psychotherapist.

So he just took her hand, and said, "I love you too, Ma. I'll be okay." Somehow. At least, he'd learn to fake it better.

"You can talk to your dad, you know. He loves you very much, and it hurts him that you won't give him a chance."

Justin couldn't suppress the snort that rose from somewhere below his pancreas. "I'm pretty sure Dad would've been much happier with identical Brandons."

"That's absolutely not true. He pushed you more when

you were younger because he knows how much you're capable of. Brandon…pushed himself."

"See? It would have been easier to have two Brandons." Justin was rethinking that plan to forgo begging for morphine. Where had that medic gone?

"If only you had a special someone here to settle down with," Mom said. "I suspect you noticed what a lovely young lady Allie's grown into."

If she only knew how much he'd noticed, how much Allie was already fucking with his drive to get the hell away from Blue Mountain and everything about this place that fed his personal hell.

Mom smiled. "Maybe you should spend some time with her before you decide definitively about your future."

"Oh God! My leg is killing me! Medic, I need drugs!"

• • •

"That Morgan boy always had a knack for ruining things." Lorena sighed as she folded her elegant limbs into the passenger side of her silver Lexus.

Since Eve was driving, Allie was left to scramble into the backseat.

"Mother, I don't think he fell down the steps on purpose." Eve put the car in gear and guided them along the winding driveway.

Allie wasn't so sure. Once he'd realized he was kissing her, he'd seemed completely disgusted and might have been willing to jump off a bridge to get away from her, but she wasn't going to share that with anyone.

"Well, at least he's going to have to stay put for a while

longer. Perhaps a month or two of convalescence will give his brain time to catch up and make him realize that he would be an idiot to turn down the position we've been holding for him. The rest of us can't continue to divide the responsibilities for managing the new brand indefinitely."

The blood in Allie's head sizzled and popped. "Things have been pretty slow down in the mail room, you know. I'd be more than happy to step up and participate."

"Here we go," Eve muttered, taking a hard left onto the main road.

Lorena's long-suffering sigh this time was worthy of a Daytime Emmy. "Sweetheart, you know you're not just the mail girl. You're the social media specialist as well, and in today's world, that's as important as being the CFO."

Allie managed to catch her snort in time to morph it into a cough. She caught Eve's cautionary glance in the rearview mirror, but as usual, ignored it. "You know, Mom, it would be important if more of Blue Mountain's drinkers were young enough to know how to use Facebook and Twitter. I bet most of them haven't even heard of Instagram. I think we need to work harder to attract younger drinkers."

From the driver's seat, Eve didn't even gasp, she just kind of gurgled.

"Allegra Louise McGrath. Trying to dismantle the status quo is no way to work your way up the ladder of success."

The rickety ladder to the moldy hayloft, more like it. "Blue Mountain needs some oomph. Some youth. Some… oh, I don't know…moonshine action."

"We're not going to have this conversation again. We've explained how your cute little idea doesn't fit with the traditional, elegant image of Blue Mountain bourbon. Moonshine capitalizes on the redneck hillbilly stereotype that we here in the Bluegrass have been trying to overcome for decades." Lorena turned in her seat to give Allie the "I'm your mother and you will hear me" face.

Allie heard—and saw—but barreled ahead anyway. "I get that, but I'm not going to sell actual moonshine, and you know that. I want to sell white dog. Raw whiskey. *Baby bourbon.* It can be fun and hip, kind of like moonshine is right now, but not as, I don't know…illegal-sounding. More snazzy bootlegger, less toothless, shoeless shotgun carrier."

The car swerved, and everyone grabbed their seats. "Sorry. Uh, I saw a possum on the road." Eve's jaw was tight.

Poor Eve. Allie had been trying for years to convince her to get some brass ovaries and cast her lot with Allie, but she refused. Eve was the peacemaker; Allie was the rebel.

The hardheaded, stubborn, relentless rebel. She got that from her dad, she knew. How many times had she heard, over the years, "Just like your dad. Get an idea in that head of yours, and you're going to follow it to the end, aren't you?"

She may have reached the point where she recognized that she wasn't going to get Blue Mountain behind her white dog idea, but she hadn't given up on the concept. She just needed to go at it from another direction. Lorena was right about one thing—Allie couldn't give up. Apparently not even after she'd had her heart stomped on and ground into the ashes of childhood melodrama. Damn that Justin Morgan!

After seeing him tonight, it was clear that her heart wasn't quite done with him.

Which Justin was she mooning over? The one she'd been in love with so long ago? The flirty boy in the cloakroom?

The forlorn warrior, still grieving the loss of his best friend? Or was there a whole different Justin in there that she was attracted to?

Her chest tightened, reminding her that it didn't matter. He was planning to leave as soon as he could, so she had no business getting attached to him again. Whoever he was, he wasn't the boy she'd grown up with, the one who'd jumped in to participate every time she came up with a new money-making scheme when she was ten.

Though this scheme wasn't that of a little girl. Rainbow Dog Whiskey had a well-thought-out business plan. And she was going to make it work.

"You can put lipstick on the plow horse, but it's not going to be the thoroughbred image we want associated with Blue Mountain Bourbon," Lorena said. "Evelyn Marie, slow down, or you're going to kill us all."

And that was the end of that conversation. Again.

· · ·

"I can't just go on a cruise and leave you here." Justin's mother all but wrung her hands over his bedside. "You've got a severe sprain. That's almost worse than a break! How are you going to get in and out of bed? The bathtub? Who's going to feed you?"

"Mom, I've been feeding myself for almost thirty years now. I know how to work the microwave and call the pizza place."

"You've got that huge brace and all those wrappings. What if something rubs and you get a bedsore that gets infected?"

"I'm not bedridden. I promise to send you leg selfies every day."

Justin's dad leaned against the wall, arms crossed over his massive chest. "It will be fine, Cathy. Justin will have plenty of time to catch up on the business and go over our ideas for 8-Ball, and come up with some plans of his own."

"That's not what—" He stopped himself. He'd fight that battle later. First he had to get rid of his parents. The idea of spending the next however many days lying on the couch sounded like hell. Having his mother hovering over him 24-7? Hell with sugar on top.

"I'm worried you're going to find a way to sneak onto a plane and go do that forest fire parachute thing before you're healed."

As appealing as that sounded, those plans were on hold. But not indefinitely. "Don't worry, I'll be here when you get back. I promise. I don't want you to miss your vacation."

His father smiled. "Come on, Cathy. We've had this trip planned for two years. Who knows what kind of trouble my parents will get into if we let them go without us?"

She scowled at her husband. "Brandon, Eve, and Lorena will be on the boat to keep an eye on them."

"Oh, no," Brandon protested from the windowsill where he sat in Justin's hospital room. "I'm not gonna be in charge of taking Grandpa to bingo. He cheats. I'll stay home with Justin."

Mom patted him on the arm. "Grandpa promises to behave. He's looking forward to taking you on some excursions while we girls have spa treatments and your dad plays shuffleboard." She tilted her head. "Tell me again why Allie isn't going?"

Clyde shrugged and looked at Brandon.

Brandon stood and fiddled with the remote for the TV. "I'm not sure. She said she's taking a class, I think."

"What kind of class? She's got more degrees than we've got barrels," Clyde said.

"I don't know," Brandon said. "But maybe if you guys would give her something more to do around Blue Mountain than play on the internet, she might use the education she's got and stop trying to overachieve."

"She's got plenty to do around Blue Mountain, she just doesn't want to do it," Clyde stated, his arms crossed. He turned his eye toward Justin. "Just like there's plenty for you to do."

"Not now, Clyde," Mom said, tapping him gently on the arm.

Justin couldn't wait for his parents to leave so he could grill Brandon about Allie's real reasons for skipping the cruise. He wasn't known for his intuitive abilities, but he'd shared a house with Brandon for the first nineteen years of his life, so he could tell with 99 percent certainty when his brother was lying.

His father opened his mouth to say something, but Mom cut him off. "That's it!" she said, her smile brighter than the day. "Allie can come stay at our house and keep an eye on you!"

Oh, hell.

"That's a great idea," Brandon said, straight-faced. That innocent look hid double-crossing trouble. Justin could feel it. If he were the suspicious type, he might suspect that Brandon had put his mother up to this. Some subtle, "Gee, Mom, it's a shame that Justin's going to be home alone, his poor, lonely, single self. And poor, lonely, single Allie is going to be right down the hill."

It really didn't matter if they'd cooked up a plan or not. No way was Allie going to stay at his house while he was helpless. "I'll be fine. Caleb can take breaks from managing things down at the distillery and check in on me. I promise to carry my cell phone everywhere I go. I'm just going to lie around and watch TV and do physical therapy. You don't have to get Allie to come."

Oh, but he'd like to get Allie to come. The memory of her in his arms last night was enough to stir him even through the fog of pain and Vicodin that clouded his brain. She was so fucking hot. And when she'd pressed her heat against his thigh, he'd nearly lost it himself.

What had he been thinking? She must have been totally wasted to have let him get her so wound up. Thank God she'd come to her senses and pushed him away, or he might have fallen to his knees, hiked that tight little skirt up and tugged the lace of that red thong aside, and—

"This will be perfect," Mom said. "I'll go call her right now." As his parents left the room, Justin pointed at his brother. "You. You can't let this happen."

"Why not?"

"Because—" He couldn't tell Brandon that he'd made out with Allie on the back porch of the country club last night. And that if she stayed at their house he wasn't sure he'd be able to keep his grubby hands off of her. And that if he put his hands on her, he'd contaminate her with the crap that ran through his head on a daily basis.

Because if he told Brandon that, he'd have to share the crap...

Justin shook his head. "Talk."

"I don't know what you mean."

"What's Allie got cooking? I don't think she's skipping a vacation just to take a class that she could take any time."

Brandon grinned and started talking. By the time he finished, Justin was nodding. He wasn't exactly sure how, but he had a feeling that this was his way to both help Allie and satisfy his promise to Dave. And maybe get his dad off his back once and for all, too.

Chapter Four

Allie let herself into the Morgan family's giant log "cabin" and tucked the key into her back pocket. She'd seen the Morgan and McGrath group off on their world cruise — at least, the airport leg of it — and was here to start the Great Justin Watch.

How had she gotten herself into this? Well, she reminded herself, she'd kissed him into diving headfirst down a stone staircase, so she kinda owed him. And then, if she hadn't managed to get the whole fam-damily out of town by agreeing to Justin-sit, she wouldn't have a chance to work on her double-secret project. As it was, she was going to have to scramble to get Rainbow Dog off the ground in time to get it ready for the On the Rocks liquor festival in Georgia week after next.

Because she was going to be busy trying to take care of a man she wasn't sure she could keep her hands off of. And playing naughty nurse was a very distracting proposition.

Like Justin was going to willingly let her do anything at all to help him. He was probably just as shocked at the idea of having her for a nursemaid as she was of being it.

She wasn't sure she could spend the next week or so avoiding talking with him, but she could probably keep things light and friendly and avoid any mention of their embarrassing encounter at the country club. It would all be okay. Really it would. They could hang out, renew their friendship, and she could purge herself of this newly reborn attraction. And maybe help lighten his load, because he was surely carrying some emotional baggage.

Unless she managed to make it worse by losing her mind and groping him or begging him to grope her. In which case she'd just convert to Catholicism and find a convent somewhere.

She tossed her laptop bag on the kitchen counter and dislodged a pile of papers.

"Crap." Allie's own mother was frighteningly anal about personal correspondence—probably a reactive measure to her father's tendency to get involved in underhanded dealings that Lorena didn't want anyone to know about—so it was weird to see a pile of mail lying around for any open eyes to fall on. Eyes that might read something like,

"Dear Sergeant Morgan, Operation Homefront would like to thank you for your generous donation of—"

"Holy crap!"

It looked like Justin had donated everything he'd made in the Marine Corps to the charity that provided emergency assistance to families of service members and wounded warriors.

She groped for a chair and plunked onto the seat, staring at the letter.

Justin had had a huge heart—that was why she'd idolized him when she was little. He'd always helped her with her moneymaking ideas, gone along with all of Dave's wild schemes, been the manual labor for all of Brandon's do-gooder Boy Scout projects... But this Justin seemed so different, so distant at times, and yet—who *was* Justin Morgan now?

Where was he?

"Justin? Where are you?"

The two-story great room was cool and empty, golden light amplified by the bare pine-log walls.

Her heart gave a little jolt of concern when she didn't hear anything. "Justin?"

Nothing.

If he'd fallen, busted his head open, and died, she was going to kill him. She hurried down the hall that led to the bedrooms. Justin's room was at the end, Brandon's was closer to the living room, and there was a bathroom in between. Their parents had a suite on the second floor, above the guys' rooms. When she was little, she'd run in and out of these rooms, playing hide-and-seek and war, and whatever other crazy game the five Morgan and McGrath kids cooked up, but it had been a good twelve years since she'd been past the living room.

Justin's door was ajar, and Allie gave it a cursory knock before pushing it open. His bed was unmade, sheets and comforter tossed to one side and half a dozen pillows arranged here and there, no doubt to support his injured leg while he slept. She'd noticed a similar mountain of pillows on the recliner in the living room.

Breathing deeply, she shivered, turned on just by standing this close to his bed. And, really, after eight years—even with a coatroom debacle, and one two-story stair stumble—she had no business reacting to this man at all. For all intents, he should be a stranger now. A man she recognized but didn't know. A man who gave all of his money to help military families in need and kissed her like there was a conduit from his lips to her power switch.

She straightened one of his pillows. The familiar smell of clean laundry was underlain with Acqua di Gio and something richer. She was surprised to realize that she could have identified the room by Justin's scent after spending those few drunken minutes wrapped in his arms. She had imprinted on him. Like those baby geese from that Jeff Daniels movie, except the baby geese hadn't wanted to roll around on Jeff Daniels's bed and touch themselves. *Okay, McGrath, move your libido away from the bed. There's nothing for you here.*

There was a prescription package from the pharmacy on the nightstand, but it didn't look like it had even been opened. Pain pills. She snorted. Tough guy. He was probably getting by on Advil and Blue Mountain Seven Year Special.

She pulled her ponytail tighter and took the phone from her pocket, ready to pull up Justin's phone number and call if she couldn't find him. Though where he'd go by himself, and how he'd get there, she had no idea.

Something white on the outside deck caught Allie's eye. She pushed open the sliding glass door and froze.

Justin lay in a chaise longue, sleeping in the warm spring

sunshine wearing nothing but a towel. One arm lay above his head, and she visually traced the line from his curled fingers, over the pale underside and dark hair of his underarm, to his chest. His pecs had always been well-developed—he and Dave had had this ridiculous push-up competition every spring, and Justin always won. He apparently hadn't let that habit slide. He was relaxed, so his abs weren't all six-packy at the moment, but he could have had a keg belly and she'd probably still want to trace the line of hair that bisected it to the top of that bath towel—and below.

His other hand rested right there, *below*.

Allie flushed. He had his hand over his…his…region. She gave herself a mental eye roll. His *cock*. She could think that word; she was an adult. Hell, she'd felt it pressing against her the other night on the patio. It was a funny word, though. Although no funnier than anything else—penis, dick, junk, rock-hard rod… Why was she standing here trying to decide what to call it, when she could be appreciating that it appeared to be happy for the attention it was getting from outside the towel?

Oh, dear. As she watched, Justin's fingers flexed slightly, and his…*cock*…grew. He stroked himself.

She stifled a whimper.

Her gaze shot to Justin's face. His eyes moved under his closed lids and his lips were parted, tongue darting out to wet them, biting his lip. She wanted to do that. Bite his lip. He was muttering, low, and then louder, "Yeah. Come on, Allie."

She nearly screeched out her surprise, but clapped a hand over her mouth in time. The last thing she wanted to do was wake him up. She was finally getting to give him a blow job, apparently, even though she was only participating in his sleep. Years of fantasizing about being on her knees in front of him, stroking, looking up into his eyes as she licked, then opened her lips and…

But now this was going to be cued on repeat in her dream repertoire.

He moaned again, arching and squeezing himself, moving his hand over the towel, pushing it out of the way.

Oh, God. It was so hard, so perfect. He brought his other hand into the action, running it across his chest, pinching a nipple.

She had to get out of here before he woke up and found her standing there, perving on him. Although maybe, if he woke up and— The phone in her hand let out a squeal and began to play "I Got You (I Feel Good)" by James Brown.

Shit.

A text from Eve, letting her know they'd all made it onto the ship.

When she looked again, Justin was sitting up, squinting, towel pulled back over his lap.

"Hey!" she said, pretending that she'd just come out onto the deck. "There you are."

"Have you been here long?" he asked, looking away from her to adjust a strap on his leg brace.

"Nope, just came in…er, out. Here. On the deck. When my phone rang." *Way to sound guilty, dumbbutt.* "How are you feeling? Did you have lunch? Can I get you any pain medicine?"

Justin rubbed his head, long fingers scratching through his hair. "No. I'm fine."

"Don't you want something to eat? I can make grilled

cheese and tomato soup. Or macaroni and cheese. Or I can see if there's any—"

"I don't want anything. You're not here to wait on me. But thanks." He tempered his short words with the world-famous panty-melting Morgan smile.

In case her panties weren't already damp. "Well, yeah, I kinda am. Here. To wait on you."

He turned up the wattage. "In that case, some caviar and a bottle of Angus's Single Barrel would be good. Buffy and Tiffany are coming over in an hour or so."

Her heart sank. "Seriously? You know someone named Buffy who hangs out with a Tiffany?" She shouldn't have been so crushed. Justin was the party king of the universe. Or at least, he had been before—

"No, I'm just screwing with you. Strippers of that caliber don't start work until way after dark, even for house calls."

"Very funny."

He laughed.

Crap. She would do better at remembering that he was a player if he didn't laugh when she teased him. She was no more "his girl" than any other female on the planet. Although he had kind of just been having a sex dream about *her*, hadn't he? No. Not. His. Girl.

"So, food?"

"No, I'm good. I really can get to the kitchen on my own when I choose to." He pointed at the crutches next to his lounge chair.

"Okay. It's not like I don't have work to do. My to-do list is a mile long." She turned toward the door to his room, but then looked back at him and couldn't resist one more remark just to torment herself. After all, she hadn't suffered enough over the past eight years? "Hey, are you planning to lie here naked all day? Because I have a lot of work, and I was thinking I could bring my laptop and keep you company. But if you're going to be flapping your johnson around, I might as well be naked, too. Except, if we're going to start the Blue Mountain Nudist Resort, we should probably see if we can find some sunscreen."

He smiled, and his eyes, as endlessly blue as the spring sky, held hers for a long moment. Then he looked away, over Blue Mountain and beyond, clearing his throat. "Actually, I was going to get cleaned up, but I couldn't get my brace off. So I came out here to wait until you got back. Do you mind helping me take a bath?" Asking her that was clearly hard for him.

Ha! It wasn't going to be a walk in the park for her. Because she was going to be in the bathroom with him. While he was the-rest-of-the-way naked. Because people didn't bathe with their clothes on. And she was going to have to find a way to keep her hands to herself.

"No problem," she said. *Oh, boy*.

· · ·

Had she noticed how fucking hard he was when she'd walked out on the deck? Justin didn't think so; she was standing in the doorway looking at her phone, so she probably hadn't seen him. He was going to go with that assumption.

He would have preferred to wait until Brandon or his dad came home in two weeks so he didn't have to ask Allie to help him bathe—except he had visions of smelling like that batch of sour mash he'd been experimenting with, but forgot about before the family left for vacation one summer.

But Christ. Waking up and seeing Allie there—he'd been having the hottest potentially wet dream of his life. Allie had been kneeling between his feet, wearing that thong, and the heels from the anniversary party, and a smile…

"Well, come on, then, let's get you de-grungified." She padded across the deck. No Victoria's Secret angel looked as hot as she did in jeans, a Blue Mountain polo shirt, and flip-flops, her tight curves just begging to be explored.

But Justin reminded himself that he was impervious to her curves, begging or otherwise, because they were off-limits.

Once, back when Allie was still sending him packages while he was deployed, Dave had teased him about it. Said he didn't want to have to kick his ass for whacking off over his little sister. Justin had looked at the photo of the round-faced, straight-hipped redhead, who looked so much like her brother at that age, and laughed. Now he tried to visualize a mental "hazardous" sign, held by an M15-wielding Dave McGrath, but the sign just added on "when wet."

And then Dave's glare got more ferocious. Justin tucked the towel around his waist and hoisted himself up onto his good leg, holding on to his crutches with one hand. Allie put a shoulder into his side and an arm around his waist. He tried not to lean on her, he really did. He tried not to put his free arm around her and smell her hair.

"Holy shit, Justin, you're heavy."

He couldn't think about her soft body beneath his, those green eyes staring up at him, all soft and wanting. He was Justin the Buddy, not Justin the Creeper. "It's because my manly muscles are extra dense. Like Superman, except instead of steel I'm a man of granite. I'm thinking of volunteering to serve as a human grain mill. It's going to be the newest thing in bourbon—whiskey made from literally hand-ground corn. My hands." He could probably use his dick, as hard as it was every time he thought of Allie on the country club patio. Or here on the back deck.

"You are the most full-of-crap person on the planet, do you know that?"

And yet she didn't pull away. If anything, her hand tightened on his waist.

"Let me go, babe. I can hobble in there under my own steam."

She let him go, but hovered close by. From the corner of his eye, he could tell she was checking him out.

He tried to gimp a little faster to keep her from noticing that his towel wasn't hanging flat in the front. "You're making me nervous," he told her.

"Good." Her grin had a hint of evil. This was good. *This* Allie he was comfortable with—the Allie he remembered as a teenager, who gave him shit and took none. It was the newer Allie, the Allie who looked at him a certain way when she thought he wasn't watching, who was the dangerous one. "You don't know if I'm going to trip you or steal your towel, do you?"

Well, hell, he hadn't thought of that.

They made it to the bathroom, and Allie turned on the faucets to fill the tub. She patted the edge, and he lowered himself to sit, his bum leg sticking awkwardly out into the room. He had to put his hand in hers to steady himself.

She knelt and began unfastening the Velcro strips holding the brace in place.

Jesus, Mary, and Uncle Steve. She was on her knees in front of him, and he was wearing a damned towel. He had a moment of dream déjà vu. A strand of rich honey hair had come loose from her ponytail and curled in the steam rising from the tub. He reached out to tuck it around his finger, but then pulled up short of actually touching her. She was Dave's kid sister. No touching.

She looked up, something like heat in her eyes that was quickly masked by humor. "Do you want some Mr. Bubble in your tub?"

He actually considered it. She was going to have to help him in and out of the tub. But he couldn't quite figure out how he was going to casually scoop a handful of bubbles over his semi-stiffy between dropping his towel and getting into the water.

It wasn't that he was overly modest. He'd actually been awarded a Most Likely to Get a Ticket for Public Nudity certificate by his unit before he left Afghanistan. But this was Allie. And he was still half hard, er, three-quarters, maybe. *Well, fuck it.* He'd already scared the crap out of her the other night. If she thought he was some kind of dirty old man, she was probably right.

He turned a little, to maneuver his good leg into the tub. He took a breath and grabbed the side of his towel, ready to yank it off.

Allie must have realized the reality of his predicament, because her face was red. She met his eyes with a stricken expression, then dropped her gaze like his groin was an eye magnet.

"It's just a dick, Sneezy," Justin said, pulling the towel off Band-Aid-style—all at once, to get the agony over with.

He lowered himself into the water while she cradled his damaged ankle.

She stared at his crotch. And kept staring.

Justin almost reached for the towel again.

"You're right. It's just a dick," she said, once he was settled. She turned to walk out. "I'm going to get started on some work. Holler when you want to get out of the tub."

"It's not *just* a dick," he called after her. "It's a really nice dick!"

Chapter Five

Allie finished the regular company data compilation quickly, so she could shift to her own project. She opened her double-secret folder and went over her plans—making sure nothing would be knocked out of alignment by one gimpy marine. Since the elders had shut her out, she was making an end run to test market Rainbow Dog Whiskey—flavored, un-aged bourbon. The distillery managers would be taking the Blue Mountain bourbon entries to the On the Rocks liquor festival, since the rest of the family was on their cruise. Brandon and Eve planned to leave the vacation a few days early to go to the awards ceremony, but everyone else would skip it this year. Thank God. Allie planned to go a day early to sneak her samples of Rainbow Dog into the competition. If all went well, she'd have an opportunity to launch her hillbilly chic product right around Blue Mountain's objections.

Looking after Justin had thrown a clinker into the works, but she was sure she'd manage to figure out something to do with him when she left for Georgia. Maybe one of his bimbo lady friends would come stay with him.

That thought gave her a stomachache, but she shoved it away and played with some fantasy sales projections.

Hitting "enter" one last time, Allie watched the number she was looking for appear in the highlighted cell on her laptop screen. "Yes!"

"Yes, what?"

Allie jumped and slapped the screen of her computer closed. "What are you doing?" She sat back, trying to pretend that she hadn't been doing anything top secret.

"That's my question. What are you working on?" Justin leaned on his crutches behind Allie's seat on the couch. She'd been so focused that she hadn't heard him drag himself into the room. But now she was aware of his breath stirring the hair on the back of her neck. Why did he have to breathe like…like…sex?

After his bath earlier, he'd claimed exhaustion and closed his door on her, saying he was going to take a nap, but Allie had heard strains of *Judge Judy* and *The People's Court* coming from his room. He was avoiding her. Which was fine, she told herself. She had work to do.

"Nothing. Just some marketing data." She turned to look at him, so she didn't have to feel him breathe his sexy breath on her. Or smell his sexy clean body. Except now she had to look at his stupid sexy face.

"Uh-huh." He shook the hair out of his eyes. Since leaving the service, he hadn't had it cut, and it grew fast. He'd be looking like a hippie in a couple of weeks if he didn't get to the barber soon. Yeah. A dirty, lazy hippie. Not a sexy boy next door aching for her fingers in his mop. She eyed his impressive shoulders, stretching the threadbare Bourbon Trail T-shirt that was more hole than fabric. "You don't wear that shirt in public, do you?"

"Only for you, Sneezy." He tilted his head. "I am, however, not as dumb as I look, and I'm not easily distracted. What are you working on?"

She hated when he called her "Sneezy." It made her feel about fourteen years old, trying to be cool and hang out with the boys while they sneaked cigarettes and hid *Hustler* magazines in the clubhouse they'd built in the woods.

When the boys were off at football practice, she'd gone in and stolen the cigarettes they hid there, breaking them in pieces to make it look like a raccoon had gotten in and torn things up.

The porn she didn't mess with though, other than, yeah, okay, maybe, to look. She'd spent some time on the internet after that, trying to find out if her own parts were normal, because she didn't look like those girls. Who knew there were so many different sizes and shapes of cooches? Of course, she'd also learned there were a lot of different sizes and shapes of penises, too. And after seeing Justin naked today, she—

"Hey, babe, my eyes are up here," Justin said, laughing.

She realized she was staring at the crotch of his knit basketball shorts and jerked her gaze to his face, but the damage was done. She was totally turned on, just from being so close to him. Again.

"I know it's amazing, but you've already had your free look for today."

Her cheeks grew hotter. "I was going to make chicken cacciatore for supper. Does that sound okay to you?" She tucked her laptop under her arm, pushed off the cushions, and started for the kitchen.

"Oh, no you don't." He reached across the back of the couch, grabbing for the computer.

She sidestepped and he got a handful of her shirt, pulling her toward him. He was at a distinct disadvantage, balance-wise, but had at least seventy-five pounds more muscle, so they fell toward each other, landing on the sofa in a pile of limbs.

"Damn!" He lay over her, bum leg between her body and the back of the couch, other knee between her own. *Oh.* His perfect, hard thigh. Right *there.*

Through the haze of lust brought about by lying in a tangle of Justin, she managed to ask, "Is your leg okay?" She had visions of explaining how she failed in her first twenty-four hours to keep Justin safe. Bad enough she'd gotten him injured in the first place; now she was knocking him down again.

"Yeah. But you do have a knack for sweeping me off my feet. Are *you* okay?"

"Well," she said, "that's an interesting question." Her laptop slid to the floor, the hand that had been holding it now on his waist. He held himself slightly above her, so his whole weight wasn't pressing her down into the couch, but impulse wanted her to pull him fully over her, wondering what it would feel like to have him collapse against her, spent after an orgasm.

Her other hand was trapped between their bodies, lower, and she realized that she was feeling…not the padded top of the brace under his gym shorts, but—she wiggled her fingers experimentally, turning her hand just enough to feel—no, that wasn't the brace.

She gasped.

"Jesus," he said. But he didn't move away, as the not-brace became not-soft.

Her own body warmed and throbbed in response. Looking up, she was shocked to see that his expression—lust and confusion—mirrored her own thoughts. Lust was edging confusion for the lead. Good sense had fallen far behind.

She stroked him. The hard length outlined against the silky fabric of his shorts allowed her to explore contours she'd admired from a distance earlier in the day, both on the deck and in the tub. "Okay," she said, hearing her voice waver. "You're right. It's a really nice dick."

The laugh that huffed from his chest vibrated against her, causing her to arch against him with a whimper.

Which he apparently misinterpreted as distress.

"Oh, shit, babe. Sorry." He struggled to move off of her, but his bad leg was wedged between her body and the couch, and she still had a firm grip on his penis.

She reluctantly released him and moved to the edge of the couch to give him room.

A few seconds and much thrashing and cursing later, they were sitting side by side, looking anywhere but at each other. Her chest tightened with embarrassment. She figured—hoped—Justin would escape back to his room, and started to rise so she could help him find his crutches.

He surprised her with a hand on her arm, and then shocked the hell out of her with his words. "We should talk about this," he said.

"Okay…"

His blue eyes shone with sincerity. "I don't want you to

feel uncomfortable around me. After…you know, after the patio the other night, and this just now… I'm not going to molest you or anything. My God, you're Dave's little sister. It's just…you know, I'm a guy. My body has a mind of its own."

Of course it did. She knew that.

Be my girl.

Justin didn't differentiate between women physically or mentally.

Looking down, she noticed a damp spot on the front of his shorts, which gave her pause, eased the mortification that her indiscriminate groping had caused. He might not want her—at least, not specifically her—but his body certainly liked her.

Annoyance flared in her chest. "Is this where you'd tell your wife, after she catches you with your secretary, 'I have needs'?" She did stand then. "I'm pretty sure I'm the grabby one in this instance. But *your* virtue is safe with *me*."

As she attempted to flounce from the room, she caught sight of his reflection in the mirror over the fireplace, and thought for a moment she saw…longing? But when she glanced back, he was shaking his head and adjusting that damned brace again.

· · ·

Dinner conversation was somewhat stilted after the near miss on the couch. Justin ate everything on his plate and asked for seconds, all the while scrambling for small talk.

Why was he struggling for something to say? He was the supreme deity of meaningless conversation. He could schmooze anyone, from a cranky Muslim shopkeeper to a crankier four-star general. He just couldn't seem to stay out of the minefield that was Allie McGrath without stepping in something.

"Do you want some iced tea?" she asked, getting up to carry their plates to the sink.

"I'd like a *drink*, if you're pouring."

"You sure you don't want iced tea?" she asked.

"Hey, it's still five o'clock somewhere."

Allie sighed. "I'm not going to turn into a nag, but you seem to be drinking a lot lately. If there's something you want to talk about—"

"Thanks, babe. I'm good. Just a little sore, and a shot of family comfort is better than any painkiller."

She nodded, apparently accepting his denial. She could probably tell that he wasn't completely comfortable at home. Hell, *everyone* could tell. He saw the worried glances, noticed the tiptoeing around. At least Allie didn't tiptoe. She practically scampered.

He was so used to the routines of military life that the casual atmosphere of home, combined with the enforced in-activity of his convalescence, made him irritable and restless. Although the scampering—that was distracting.

Drinking, however, was more than distracting. A shot or three took the edge off, blurred the discomfort of reality. He'd ease up as soon as he got the hell out of here—away from his perfect brother and the overambitious expectations of his father—and got to work out West.

He refused to consider—especially since Brandon and Clyde weren't even in Crockett County at the moment— that adding alcohol to his bloodstream was an attempt to neutralize the ardor simmering in his body. He could not go there. He'd promised Dave he'd watch out for Allie, not compromise her virtue.

"Are you going to go down to the distillery tomorrow?" Allie set a glass with about a quarter of the recommended dose of bourbon in front of him. "I've got to deliver some paperwork and check on…something. If you want to go down and see the new rickhouse, I can drive you."

Justin dreaded going to the distillery. He'd managed to avoid it since coming home. Seeing all of those little bottles of Dave's 8-Ball had nearly destroyed him the other night at the anniversary party. Seeing Dave's dream project finished—that might do him in completely. But staying here, with nothing to do but try to keep his hands off Allie, wasn't an option. And he needed to snoop around. He had to figure out what the hell she was up to with her flavored white dog project. Brandon's explanation the other day in the hospital sounded a little wonky. Of course, that could have been the pain meds.

"Yeah, I'll go. Do Caleb and Sherry need help getting shit ready for On the Rocks?"

Caleb and Sherry, the middle-aged married couple who lived on the Blue Mountain grounds, conducted tours of the distillery and ran the little café that sat inside the gates of the plant.

Blue Mountain's entry into the tourism business had been another of Dave's brilliant ideas. He said he didn't have anything else to think about while on patrol in Afghanistan, so he came up with ideas and emailed them home to Brandon, who sorted through the dumbass ones (like sponsoring a bourbon-tasting fund-raiser for Little League baseball teams to promote the idea that bourbon should be a part of every activity from the earliest age) and occasionally implemented something that might have a shot of working.

"Yeah, they're ready for On the Rocks," Allie said. She'd come around the table and handed Justin his drink, but in her other hand, she carried her laptop. She put it on the table, tapping it nervously. "But I was thinking. Maybe you and I should go, instead of Caleb and Sherry."

. . .

"Yeah, right." Justin's voice echoed into his bourbon. He took a drink, then put the glass down carefully on the table. Wiping at his mouth with the side of his hand, he pushed his chair back.

In spite of his definite lack of enthusiasm, it was now or never. Sometime between trying to keep her project from Justin and almost having an orgasm from touching his genitals, she'd decided to share her secret. She put her computer in front of him and opened the screen. She took a deep breath and stepped behind him. "Just watch this, okay?"

After a few seconds, the screen brightened, and the media player appeared. Bluegrass music accompanied video of the rolling hills of western Kentucky, water bubbling over limestone rocks in the Blue Mountain River, and Thoroughbred colts frolicking in green fields surrounded by dark brown fences.

Justin shot a look at Allie as her own voice replaced the music.

She cringed to hear herself, but was proud of the words she'd put together, a testament to the good people of

Kentucky and the fine bourbon tradition of corn, barley, rye, and wheat whiskey, aged in new, charred oak barrels, and the excellence of Blue Mountain Bourbon's long-standing history in the region.

Then the music changed to a country rap song, accompanying video of a NASCAR race, interspersed with laughing, beautiful people riding around in beat-up trucks.

And then her voice again introducing Blue Mountain's Rainbow Dog Whiskey—cherry-flavored Red Dog, apple-flavored Green Dog, and a berry Blue Dog, among others.

After the video ended, Justin picked up his glass and stared into the amber liquid, swirling it a little.

"Well? What do you think?" She bit at a hangnail, trying not to bounce while she waited for his reaction.

"What are you trying to do?" he finally asked.

"I want us to jump into the future with both feet. Moonshine is hot. Between reality TV and shows like *Justified*, Greater Appalachia is cool as hell. Have you seen Daryl on *Walking Dead*? He's like the sexiest redneck ever."

He raised an eyebrow. "Greater Appalachia?"

Allie shrugged. "If it's not a thing, I'm going to make it a thing. I've done a ton of research. We have the capacity to get into the market." She leaned over his shoulder, inadvertently flattening her breast against his back, and sending her nipple on a fact-finding mission. Ignoring her hormones, she hit a couple of keys and pulled up a slide show presentation with her financial projections.

"We can use Dave's and your raw 8-Ball recipe, if you'll sign off on it. Then the old farts can't accuse me of illegally diverting perfectly good fetal Blue Mountain bourbon. If we fired up that old pot still you and Dave used to make

8-Ball, we could have enough distilled and bottled up to take to On the Rocks. There are a bunch of distributors open to carrying moonshine, and if you'll go and be the face of—"

Justin held up a hand to cut her off. "Stop."

"But—"

He leaned forward and twisted around, so she had to straighten and step away from him to see his face. "What do the 'rents say?"

"Um, well…" Crap. The side of her thumb went back into her mouth while she decided what to tell him.

"Leave that alone," he said, pulling her hand away from her lips. "You've shown this to them, right?"

"Yeah." She shoved her hands into her pockets to keep from gnawing them bloody.

Justin stared at her, eyebrow raised.

She sighed and felt her shoulders slump. "I brought it up at the last board meeting, but the old people wouldn't even consider it. Said the Blue Mountain name is all about tradition and exclusivity, Keeneland and country clubs. Selling white dog would be like bootlegging moonshine, and to quote my dear mother, 'We do not engage in white-trash activities.'"

"What did Brandon and Eve say?"

"You know how they are. They like it, but neither one of them would say 'shit' if they had a mouthful. Eve's so busy trying to stay one step ahead of our mother, she doesn't pay attention to anything but keeping the books straight. Brandon likes it, but he doesn't have any power to make decisions. He says maybe after the new rickhouse is up and stocked, we can try some, send it out to local businesses, but I think we need to go bigger. We need to get it out nationally, because the local markets are sort of saturated. Send it out West. L.A., Vegas. Heck, San Francisco. Shake up the wine snobs a little."

Justin was listening, nodding, so she kept going. "We're scheduled to start barreling up Dave's batch to become 8-Ball bourbon in three days. But if you'll help me, we can use part of that to make Rainbow Dog flavors and have it ready to take to Georgia."

Allie usually didn't know enough to quit when she was ahead, so she figured she'd probably overshot the mark a little. But he was nodding. "Dave's stuff is supposed to be the first bourbon aged in the new rickhouse."

Justin picked up his glass again, put it to his nose, and breathed deeply. Then he tilted the glass, draining the shot of 8-Ball. He stood, shoving the crutches under his arms. "I don't think so," he said, as he hopped around her and out of the kitchen.

Chapter Six

Justin woke with a nose full of vanilla and chocolate, and a head leaking brain cells. He eyed the empty fifth of bourbon on his nightstand. Well, at least he hadn't fallen asleep curled around it like the stuffed bunny someone — his mother, probably — had pulled from the closet as a welcome-home gesture. He'd tossed the threadbare beast, which only had half of one ear and more closely resembled the Taco Bell Chihuahua than a rabbit, onto the chair next to the bed, where it sat glaring at him, accusation clear in its button eyes.

What did the goddamned thing know about how it felt to try to sleep here, where the night was so quiet that the nightmares had room to breed and grow? The bourbon didn't stop them from coming, but at least they were fuzzier when he woke up. "Don't fucking judge me, Hoppy."

"What did he do to you?"

"Shit!" Justin jerked around at the sound of a female voice, then put a hand on the top of his head to keep it from falling off.

Allie stood in the doorway, holding a plate of cookies and a glass of milk. "Butter and sugar. It's what's for breakfast," she said, coming in and handing him the food.

"Thanks, I think," he said, taking a bite of Toll House awesomeness. The smudge of flour on her right breast momentarily distracted him from his hangover, but then he eyed the milk, and his stomach lurched. "I don't suppose I can have a glass of water?" he asked.

She didn't comment on the empty whiskey bottle as she went into his bathroom, dumped the milk in the sink and turned on the faucet. She rinsed the glass and refilled it, then carried it back to him. After handing it to him, she paused, then reached for something on the nightstand.

"Is this Dave's watch?"

Fuck. "Yeah."

She rubbed the face with her thumb, fiddled with the straps. "I'm glad you have it."

Justin's chest burned. He swallowed as much water as he could to avoid responding.

"He loved this," she said, laying it on her own wrist and holding it in place. "He said it was as badass as a wristwatch could be."

"Put it back," he snapped, before he could slap a gag order on his inner asshole.

But she nodded and laid it carefully back on the nightstand. "Are you going to the plant today?"

"I don't know. My leg's kind of—"

"Because if you're not, it would be cool if you put your marine stuff on and came with me."

"Huh?" He scratched his head. The sugar was starting

to move into his bloodstream, but he'd done some serious brain damage with the liquor last night and wasn't quite up to speed. "Where are you going?"

Allie walked across the room and opened the shades. As she bent to pull up the window sash, he admired the way she filled out the jeans she'd painted on. She wore white sneakers and a red-white-and-blue striped T-shirt that rode up a little in the back, exposing the waistband of her thong, and a curlicue thing with leaves and…

"Do you have a tramp stamp?"

She jerked up and pulled her shirt down in the back. "I prefer to call it a thong accent."

Justin snorted. "No you don't."

She shrugged, then grinned. "I really call it 'pissing off Lorena.'"

Laughing, Justin grabbed his head. "Ow. Don't make me laugh. It's too early."

"It's twelve thirty," Allie said.

"Oh, shit. Really?"

"Yeah, really. You need to get moving. I want to drop off some paperwork at the plant, and then I'm due at the VA."

His stomach dropped. He picked up his phone and checked the date. "Why are you going to the VA?"

"It's David's birthday. I volunteer at the long-term care unit there a couple of days a week anyway, but on his birthday, I take in cookies, talk to the old guys. It would be cool if you came with me. They've heard me talk about David—and you—so much. I'm sure they'd love to meet you."

"I don't know. I think I'd better check on the rickhouse, do that inventory Brandon asked me to do." He'd rather have dental work, but even going to the distillery sounded better than the VA. He was still processing her suggestion that they use Dave's 8-Ball whiskey for her Rainbow Dog thing. *Rainbow Dog. Christ.* Almost as cute as she was.

Allie sighed. "Yeah. Okay." Her disappointment in him didn't help his hangover any.

Nor did it get him any closer to figuring out how—or even whether—he should help her with her business. Though the way he'd acted last night, he sure hadn't set up any expectations that he would.

. . .

Justin waited until Allie drove away before he asked Caleb for the keys to the golf cart.

"Do you want me to drive you somewhere, son?" the distillery manager asked.

Caleb had been working at Blue Mountain as long as Justin could remember and had bailed the younger Morgans and McGraths out of many dumbass scrapes that should have gotten them in hot water with their parents. His wife, Sherry, had served the same purpose for the girls. Brandon had mentioned that she'd even dropped Allie off "for coffee" at a Starbucks a block from a family planning clinic when she'd decided she wanted to get birth control.

Justin tried not to wonder who Allie had tagged to be her first. Brandon hadn't said, and at the time, he hadn't really cared. But now he hoped that whomever she'd been with had treated her the way she deserved, like a fucking goddess.

"I'll ride with you," Caleb insisted, brow furrowed.

"No, I'm good. Thanks." He took the keys and crutched out through the front door of the business office. Braced leg propped on the front end of the cart, he waved, then drove over the hill behind the bottling facility. The vehicle whizzed along the gravel path toward the new rickhouse that rose, tall and stately, a quarter mile farther east of its sister structure. Some people thought the buildings looked like prisons, with their tall, plain brick or stone walls, narrow windows on each level, sitting out in the middle of a field. When Justin decided he wouldn't stay in Crockett County to be part of Blue Mountain Bourbon, he'd sung "Rickhouse Rock" all the way to the marine recruiting station. His father hadn't been amused.

But if he thought of the storage buildings as prisons, why was he drawn to this one?

It looked out of place, its shiny newness unsullied by the extreme variations in Kentucky weather. Justin wondered how it would change from year to year, as the sun, wind, snow, and rain heated and cooled the building, as the bourbon moved in and out of the oak, gathering flavor over the years. But then he reminded himself that he didn't care, that he really only liked bourbon for the effect, and that he wasn't going to be here to see it happen.

He maneuvered the golf cart to stop a few yards from the big front door, over which was a sign reading, RICKHOUSE 2: DANGEROUS DAVE'S DEN.

Damn. Rickhouse 1 was named "Jamie McGrath's Clubhouse" in honor of Allie and Eve's late father, who'd died in a car accident when he was much too young.

After taking his crutches from the seat next to him, Justin hoisted his pack over his shoulder and made his way to the door. He hesitated, not sure he was brave enough to enter. It was silly. Dave had never even seen this building.

The families had broken ground the day they came home from Arlington, to honor Dave in a way he would have appreciated. Justin had gone right back to war. Not to honor Dave, but to avoid facing their families' grief for as long as possible.

What would Dave have thought of Allie's Rainbow Dog idea? On one hand, he was a fan of bigger, better, bolder business, but he was also a traditional guy, trying to convince people everywhere they went to try Blue Mountain bourbon. Or any bourbon that was available.

When their buddies in the Corps went to bars and ordered scotch, or—gasp!—tequila or vodka, Dave would buy them a shot of bourbon and offer a lesson in tasting. Of course, it didn't take long for their friends to start ordering anything *but* bourbon just to get Dave to buy them a shot. Dave didn't care. He wanted everyone to love Kentucky as much as he did.

Entering the dark warehouse, Justin found a couple of new barrels sitting against the wall and hoisted himself onto one, putting his backpack on the one next to it.

He breathed in, the scent of new construction overpowering the fainter angel's share—whiskey seeping through the pores of the few barrels that had already been filled and put up. In a few months, when more racks contained filled barrels, the smell would be stronger. But by then his leg would be healed, and he would be out West, following his dream, saving forests and not all twisted up with Allie and her Rainbow Dog.

He unzipped the backpack and pulled out a new fifth of 8-Ball and a couple of Cuban cigars. He also had Dave's black dive watch, which he took out and sat on the barrel.

He wouldn't wear it, even though Dave had made him swear he'd take it with him if he died. "Don't let them bury me with that, man. It cost too damned much to rust underground. You take it and use it." Justin couldn't bring himself to wear it—the watch had killed Dave, and it was Justin's albatross, but he'd dug it out of his seabag and put it on his nightstand. He'd pack it away again and keep it safe later.

He tucked one unlit cigar in his mouth and put one next to the watch, for Dave, and cracked the seal on the bottle.

"Since you can't be here, dude, I'll have to enjoy it for you," he said to the watch. "But we can't smoke in here, so just imagine, okay?"

He pulled the cigar from his lips and took a hit of the liquor, put the cigar back, sat and stared at the rafters. Then he repeated the process, but the tightness in his chest didn't ease. He thought of Dave, how he had struggled for his last breaths to exact the promise Justin was struggling to fulfill.

The watch glared at him. "Stop giving me the business, asshole. I'm trying to look out for Allie, but she's making it damned difficult." He hoped Dave couldn't see his real thoughts about her. How fucking much he wanted her, but… "She's become quite a woman, dude. I'm not sure what you want me to do for her. She's got this crazy booze project she seems to want my help with. It's a good idea, actually, but I don't think she should be using the white dog made for your 8-Ball."

He slugged back another shot of the finished version, looked at the label. *A Justin Morgan and David McGrath recipe.*

Huh. It *was* half his recipe. He could let Allie use it for her Rainbow Dog project if he wanted to. His name was on the brand and probably on the paperwork. Hell, he never paid much attention, as long as they didn't ask him to put on a tie or show up to actually work.

He stroked his chin. This might just be the ticket to pissing the old man off enough to let him go without claw marks. Maybe a few figurative bruises, but…

• • •

Allie stopped at the office when she got back from the VA to see if Justin was still there, or if he'd gotten a ride back up the hill to his house.

"He took the golf cart a while ago," Sherry told her. "Caleb said he was going to check out Number 2, but I haven't seen him since. Maybe he drove the cart back up to the house."

"I'll go see if he's still there." She was surprised Justin had gone there without being held at gunpoint. He seemed so reluctant to get involved with anything to do with the business.

"He looked kind of sad," she said. "I bet he's missing your brother, isn't he?"

Allie had a shiver of foreboding. Justin *was* sad about David, although he'd sooner die than admit it. The shiver turned into a cold fist around her heart. *Would* he rather die than live without his best friend? And he'd given away all of his money…

Justin was unhappy here, and Dave's birthday was no doubt making it doubly difficult to cope. And as much as he chafed at the comparison, he was his father's son—and would sooner gouge out an eye than admit to feeling weak.

She ran out of the office to her truck and took off.

The rickhouse was dark in the waning daylight, but the golf cart sat nearby.

Allie stepped out of the truck and waited for a moment. What was she going to find in there?

"Are you just going to stand out there, or are you coming in here to toast Dave a happy birthday?"

Startled, she peered into the faint glow coming from the building and made out the shadowed form sitting on a barrel, bum leg propped on another.

"I didn't know Dave was in there with you. I figured he was busy giving Saint Peter a lesson in barrel rotation." Entering, her eyes adjusted to the dim yellow light of a desk lamp someone had left near the door, a remnant of the construction crew's makeshift office.

Justin swayed when she took the bottle, but caught himself before he toppled over, thick forearms braced on his thighs. His good leg was cocked to the side for balance, and there was space between his legs. If she stepped forward a foot or so...

She tipped a shot down her throat, coughed, and wiped her eyes.

"Easy, babe. Don't overdo it. Don't wanna wind up pukin' on your shoes."

"Seriously? How wasted are you?" She started to step back, but—

"Pretty wasted." He reached and caught her around the waist, pulling her between those hard thighs. Even drunk, he had a magnetism she was too weak to resist. "Babe, you are fine."

Her lips parted, ready to taste the whiskey on his, and

she felt a whisper of his breath against her. Then sanity kicked her in the butt. She wanted him, but not like this. He didn't even know who she was.

Stepping back, she sighed and reached for his crutches. "Come on, slick. Let's get back to the house."

"Shit. You're right. Dave would be so pissed off…"

Allie stamped her foot, but she didn't scream. That would have been childish. "David. Is. Not. Here."

Justin pulled back, standing straight, holding his crutches, and balanced on his good leg. "I know." He appeared very sober. Eyes narrowed, focused on her; she knew then that he knew exactly who she was.

She wasn't some random girl he'd picked up in a bar; she was the little sister of his grief, of his hard memories. "I'm here. You're here. And that's okay."

She stalked toward him. He was still by the barrel he'd been sitting on, so she pushed him back onto it and wrapped her arms around his neck, pushed herself between his legs, and pressed her breasts against his chest.

Against his soft, chiseled lips, she said, "We. Are here. Now kiss me."

And he kissed her.

Holy shit, did he kiss her.

After about half a second of shocked awareness, his lips parted, his tongue slipped out to touch her lower lip, and then his mouth was opening over hers, consuming, taking everything she was giving.

Tongues tangling, lips brushing, teeth scraping, he held her tightly against him, one big hand on her backside, one in her hair.

Gasping, she tore her mouth away from his. Staring

straight into his shell-shocked gaze, she said, "Thank you."

He didn't respond, just dropped his head and stared at the watch.

"Come on, let's get you home."

"I'm not ready to go," he told her, shaking his head.

"Justin. Come on. I'm tired, and I'm not leaving you here."

She reached for his crutches again, but was shaking so hard from emotion and arousal that she knocked over the remaining half bottle of whiskey onto the desk lamp, which shattered, sending sparks onto the stream of liquor, which ignited into a blue-white flame.

Such a small, nearly colorless fire that spread so quickly to the liquor-soaked wood of the barrel.

Allie leaped into action, grabbing a fire extinguisher from the wall and turning it on the flames, but the fire moved too fast.

"Here, I'll go get the other one," she said, handing it to Justin and sprinting down the aisle to get one from the next row.

But when she returned, she noticed a barrel of whiskey leaking fuel onto the other barrels. It was time to get out.

"Come on," Justin said, waving Allie around him with a crutch while still spraying the fire.

She'd stepped through the doorway toward the fresh, cool air, then rushed back inside, calling over her shoulder, "You go. I've got to get Dave's watch."

Chapter Seven

Dave's watch. Justin had forgotten it while he was kissing Allie.

The world slowed down and sped up simultaneously.

Allie's scream yanked Justin into the smoke behind her, his injured leg a barely perceptible obstacle.

Even with the liquor spinning through his head, he realized he was about to be responsible for her death now, too. "Dammit, Dave, I promised you. I *will* take care of her."

He limped into the smoke, shouting, "Allie! Allie, goddammit!" His heart was the only thing he could hear. His heart and the flames. And then…

"Here!"

Appearing through the thickening smoke, she was the most beautiful thing he'd ever seen. An Irish Valkyrie. The flames that had engulfed a few barrels were reflected in her eyes, and her already-burnished hair glowed. She grinned, holding that fucking watch in the air.

He wanted to throttle her. "You gotta get out of here,"

he tried to yell, but it sounded like a whisper in the heat and smoke.

"I couldn't let you lose that watch," she said, then her eyes widened. "Look out!"

He grabbed her arm and turned with her, shoving her toward the door, but wasn't able to completely avoid the wooden beam that crashed down onto his torso.

"Justin!" She was back, tugging at him.

"Get the fuck out, Allie!"

"Not without you!"

One look at her face told him she wasn't leaving.

For fuck's sake. No way was he going to run into Dave at the pearly gates carrying Allie and try to explain this. He heaved and shoved at the beam, and when he was free, he stood and pulled her against him.

Together, they limped through the smoke and out into the fresh, clean air.

He didn't realize how badly he'd been banged up until he couldn't catch his breath. "Get away from here, Allie. We're out. Go on to the truck."

"Where are your crutches?"

"I don't know." He didn't tell her that the throbbing agony in his leg was second to his crushing inability to breathe.

"Okay, I'll be right back." She left him long enough to pull the golf cart closer.

She was on her phone, calling it in, before she got to him, then helped him onto the seat. He managed to grunt loudly only once when she put her arm around his waist to support him.

"The fire department should be here soon," she assured him as she drove them back toward her truck.

"Damn," Justin panted. When the golf cart stopped next to her truck, he pulled up his shirt.

"Whoa."

His chest was red where the beam had landed on him, the edges of the board clearly visible.

"That's gonna leave a mark," she said and reached to stroke his skin.

For the moment, adrenaline took the edge off the pain when he sucked in a breath at her tender touch, but tomorrow was going to suck.

"Are your ribs broken?"

"I don't think so, just bruised." He hoped.

Smoke poured from the upper window of the rickhouse now. He didn't know if the whole place would go up in flames, but it was going to be a mess, and there was nothing they could do now but wait for the fire department. The walls were brick, but the racks inside were wooden.

Allie looked behind her, where Justin stared, then back at him. "I'm sorry."

"You're sorry?"

"For, uh, starting that fire."

"I was the drunk in the barn. I shouldn't have had that shitty lamp on anywhere near alcohol." *Good*. Remind them both, early and often, that it was a mistake. Unfortunately, it was a major screwup. "Fuck. I'm never going to get away from this place, am I? I'm going to spend the rest of my life paying for this."

Her expression softened. Putting a hand on either side of his face, she pulled his attention to her. "It's okay. It's insured. But dammit, Justin, if you die, who am I gonna make a fool of myself over?"

And she kissed him again. Pressed her smoky, sooty lips to his, and kissed the ever-loving hell right out of him. He felt her tongue brush his lips, and after a moment, he opened his mouth to her. He chased her tongue with his own, licking at her mouth, biting her fat bottom lip. His arms went around her, pulling her soft body against his hard, miserable self.

He probably would have laid her on the seat and started ripping at her clothes if a loud crash hadn't interrupted them. They jerked apart, staring at each other for a moment, before turning to see the south wall of the rickhouse collapse inward.

"Oh, shit." Allie held on to his hand, and he didn't pull away like he knew he should. He'd fucked up, big-time, and he needed to stand up and deal with what he'd done. After a moment that lasted too long, at least for a mistake that wasn't going to happen again, Justin pulled his hand out of her grasp.

. . .

The fire department arrived, and the chief himself came. EMTs checked out Allie's breathing, Justin's breathing, Justin's leg, his chest, and a long scratch Allie'd managed to gouge into her upper arm. Once she knew it was there, it hurt like a bitch, but until that point, she hadn't been aware of it.

All she could think about was the feel of Justin's lips against hers, his hand, tentatively on her waist and then sliding more confidently around her, pulling her against him.

She looked at him now, hours later, silhouetted against the floodlights that had been erected to spotlight the burned building so the firemen could check for hot spots. He hunched over his crutch, barely holding himself upright as he spoke with Sheriff Baker. But he wouldn't sit down, not even on the front seat of the golf cart, until the first responders were gone.

Her phone vibrated against her leg and she pulled it from her pocket. Finally. The insurance agent was returning her call.

"How much damage?" he asked, after the preliminary "is everyone okay?" stuff was out of the way.

"We won't know for sure until the contractor comes by in the morning, but one of the walls partially collapsed, and they're definitely going to have to rebuild a big part of the interior."

It was quiet on the other end.

"We're covered, though, right?"

The agent coughed. "It's complicated. I should probably speak with your mother or Justin's dad about this, as they were involved in purchasing the rider to the regular policy for the—"

"Are we covered or not?" Allie ground out. Jesus, even the damned insurance agent treated her like she was twelve.

A wave of warmth surrounded her as Justin neared, his body blocking the chilly spring wind.

"You're covered," the agent finally said. "But you've got a significant deductible."

When he told her the amount, Allie was more grateful than ever that Justin was nearby, because she needed to grab his crutch to keep from collapsing.

After promising to have the contractor call him, Allie said good-bye and hung up.

"How bad?" he asked. "How much is the deductible?"

"Almost as much as I have set aside to launch Rainbow Dog."

"No."

"Yep."

"Fuck."

"Yep."

"I'm going to have to sell a kidney. And a testicle."

She raised an eyebrow.

"I don't have any money. I, uh, donated—"

"I know." She waved him off. "That was really…cool." Leaving the feasibility of testicular transplants alone for the moment, she said, "It was mostly my mistake. I'll put on my big-girl panties and deal with it."

One corner of his mouth almost twitched. But then he said, "No, we were both in that warehouse, and we both know we're not supposed to be in there, uh, screwing around. I can find my Captain America Underoos, too."

She let him off the hook by not pointing out that they hadn't gotten to the screwing-around stage, but his point was made. They needed to fix this without going to their families for help. "I told you. I've got the money."

"And this isn't just your problem."

Allie chewed her bottom lip. "I have an idea." She told him.

Justin looked at her sideways. "I'm afraid to ask."

She grinned. "You're going to have to get your social butterfly personality back out and dust it off," she told him. "We're going on a road trip."

"Ah, hell," he said, finally sitting down.

Chapter Eight

The morning shone bright and happy through his parents' kitchen without a single sympathy cloud for Justin and his messed-up life. And, yes, all of the problems of yesterday could be laid solely at his feet. Contrary to whatever Allie wanted to suggest.

He'd let his grief, his misery, and ultimately, his inability to keep his hands off of her endanger the entire Blue Mountain legacy. It could be worse than it was; it could be much worse…he could have blown up Rickhouse Number *One*—and a lifetime's worth of bourbon—or someone could have died. But still, he'd been drunk, he'd been sloppy, and he'd fucked up. And he didn't give a shit about the place for himself—he'd always been about rebellion and avoiding getting stuck here—but the people he cared about still loved it, so it mattered.

And he was supposed to be watching out for Allie, not groping her every chance he got. The fire was clearly Dave warning him to keep his dick in his pants around her.

Allie, whom he'd sworn to protect, to honor her dead brother's wish to "look out for her—her heart is too big to stay away from idiots," when he knew all along that *he* was the idiot she needed protection from.

Because, *damn*. Her body called to his 24-7. And it wasn't just her body. Her quick wit and sense of humor brought him back from the brink of self-pity almost as often as he crept out on the edge.

Fuck. He had to stay away from her. But how was he going to keep his distance when she'd decided that they were going to spend the next two weeks working together, and then travel together—in his parents' motor home no less—halfway across the country to sell Rainbow Dog whiskey?

She sat across the kitchen table from him now, laying out a plan that would get Rickhouse Two on the road to recovery before anyone knew what hit it—and get her business off the ground at the same time.

"Okay. Here's the deal," she said, pushing a mug of steaming black coffee his way, then sitting down with a pad of paper. "My first plan was to show the old folks what a great idea Rainbow Dog is, and the Blue Mountain board would decide to let me make it an official brand of the distillery."

"They didn't go for that one, I'm guessing."

"Didn't even make it out of the starting gate. Option two. Use my savings to start the business."

"You have that much?" He was surprised. That was a lot of jack.

"I've got some money. Insurance payout stuff," she said, not looking at him.

Right. Her dad had left her and Eve some money.

"And that's what we're going to use for the deductible?"

"Yep. I'm gonna lend you half—with interest"—she passed him a sheet of paper with some numbers on it—"and you're going to pay me back when you get to the land of firefighting helicopter divers."

"Smoke jumpers." He sat back. She'd really thought this through. Except… "So what money are you going to use to start up Rainbow Dog?"

"That's where our road trip comes in. After you sell me some of the Dangerous Dave white dog"—she gave him a meaningful stare—"we'll make some sample product. I've been on the internet this morning booking us meetings all the way from here to Atlanta. We're going to find an investor. Someone who will be a silent partner and provide the capital—with a healthy rate of return—on an up-and-coming business venture."

"You got any candidates?" Justin asked.

"A few ideas, but nothing firm. I think if we can prove there's some interest in the product from vendors—and drinkers—we have a shot with some of the bigwigs who'll be in Georgia."

"And what if that doesn't work?"

She waved him off. "There's always plan C. Or D. Whatever. It'll be fine."

Justin thought about it for a minute. He had the authority to sell her the white dog, because even though he didn't want to be, he was on the Dangerous Dave brand paperwork. So that would be free and clear of the Blue Mountain label. Dad would be annoyed, but he couldn't…arrest him, or anything. So getting the product together was no problem. They had enough money left over from the deductible for that. The rest of it? He wasn't sure. He wished he had her confidence. What would happen if she didn't get the silent partner to invest? She'd probably just shrug and say it would take longer than she expected and act like she didn't care.

He made a decision though, there and then. No fucking way was he going to let her sacrifice her dream. He could call his dad now, throw himself on the man's mercy, and pledge to always work for Blue Mountain if his dad would cover his debt, and maybe somehow convince him to back Rainbow Dog. As if Clyde had ever thought any of Justin's ideas were worth a dime.

Or he could help Allie with her plan. Give her a chance to prove she could pull this off. Do something that would make Dave proud of him, and piss his father right the hell off.

He'd do this because he'd promised Dave he'd help her, but also because his honor—such as it was—wouldn't let him take her money to pay for the deductible. And if her plan worked, then his own plan B—go to his father with his hat in his hand—would never have to see the light of day.

"Okay, when do we leave?" he asked.

"Really? Okay?" Her big green eyes searched his, looking for a "but" that he didn't offer.

"Why not?" His brain was already working ahead, wondering if he knew anyone who might have the investment capital for something like this. Someone who would appreciate the idea and be willing to take a chance.

"Wow. I guess…if we leave in a few days, that will give us time to get some preliminary things done here, like bottle up that next batch of white dog that's due to come off the mash tomorrow, and get all of our paperwork together, that sort of thing." She stood and tugged at the legs of her jeans, which had bunched into the crease between thigh and—

Justin groaned.

"Are you okay? I bet you're sore today, aren't you?" Allie's eyes were on him, the green flecked with gold this morning.

"I'm fine." But he wasn't. He'd lain awake all night, replaying his idiocy, beating himself with his own stupidity. Sober, too, after his failed toast to his dead friend. Staying dry might seem like a good idea on the surface, if he had any hope of making decent decisions, but he'd never been one for good choices. At least if he was drunk, he wouldn't hate himself so much for fucking up.

Well, he'd hate himself anyway, but he'd still abstain.

"Can I have some more coffee?" he asked. He hated that he had to ask her to do so much for him. Then thought of asking her to do more. Or better yet, her asking him for more...

"Here you go," she said, thunking the stoneware mug on the table in front of him, bringing her scent along, confusing his senses. She pushed the sugar bowl over. "What are you smiling about?"

"Huh? I was smiling?"

"Yeah." She sat back down, chin on hand, staring at him. "What were you thinking about? I need some good news."

I was thinking about what a smart, beautiful woman you've turned out to be, and how much I'm going to enjoy spending the next couple of weeks with you. "I was thinking about how small that motor home is, and how much I hope you don't mind that I'm bringing Tiffany and Buffy."

She threw a roll of paper towels at his head.

• • •

"Here." Allie dropped a shopping bag onto Justin's stomach. "Get dressed. We're going out."

"What?" He sat up, rubbing the sleep from his eyes. His shaggy hair was charmingly smushed on one side, and she shook her head to dislodge the image of long weekend naps followed by long weekend sex. The bag fell to the floor, spilling a bright green sweatshirt onto the braided rug. "What is this?"

"It's a Crockett County High sweatshirt," she said. "What else on God's green earth comes in that color?"

Justin held the shirt up. "You gave this to me because…?"

"Because we're going to the Crockett Rockett Alumni Fund-Raiser tonight."

"Why would we want to do that? I graduated from that school. I paid my dues."

"Hence the term 'alumni.' And Blue Mountain might be the biggest taxpayer in the county, but it makes sense to show a little more goodwill to the neighborhood and support the construction of the new gym. And we have a product to promote."

She started to unload the bags of supplies she'd picked up at the craft store.

"What's all that?"

"Our contribution to the silent auction."

"We're auctioning off shredded paper and plastic wrap?"

"Yes. And just so it doesn't look stupid, I'm going to throw in a few jars of Rainbow Dog."

"Ah. Good thinking. Although I bet that shredded paper

shit brings in the bids all on its own."

She sprinkled a handful over his head. "Just go get dressed. Please?"

"Fine," he said. "But I'm not changing my socks. I need some armor against the hordes of perimenopausal female alums. Those little gals can wear a boy out."

She hefted a jar this time, but he disappeared before she could decide whether chucking it at him would be worth the time spent sweeping up the mess.

Chapter Nine

"Dude, that's Justin Morgan. He was the quarterback who took the Rocketts to state in the early '00s." For a moment, Justin thought the discussion he was overhearing centered on some other Justin Morgan. He barely remembered the one who'd played football at Crockett County High School.

"Dude. We should get him to come to spring practice. He looks like he could still throw pretty far."

"I don't know. When they get that old, they start having to get their shoulders replaced and shit."

He slowed his steps, scanning the crowd rumbling with conversation that had him disoriented. Allie turned and smiled encouragingly at him. Did she recognize that he had morphed into something that didn't belong in this environment? He took a breath and squared his shoulders. He could stand it for a couple of hours.

"That sucks. I bet getting all that metal in your shoulder sets off all kinds of metal detectors."

He didn't correct their assumptions that he had age-related bionic parts.

"That chick he's with is pretty hot."

Justin glared at the speakers, who were much younger versions of himself, wearing Rocketts football jerseys and serving hors d'oeuvres to the guests.

He shot Allie a look to see if she heard, but she had her head bent to listen to a little old lady with purple-tinged curls. She tucked a strand of hair behind one ear, exposing her long, lovely neck to his view. Much more appealing than remembering that he wasn't *from* here anymore.

He tried to look away, but was arrested at her backside, made that much more delicious when she straightened, arching her back a little.

"It's so nice to see you, Mrs. Hatchet. I can't believe you retired! Surely you have another fifteen or twenty years to go before you're old enough to collect your pension."

Mrs. Hatchet, who was ninety if she was a day, slapped her on the arm. "Smart-ass. I should give you detention." She turned her eagle eye on Justin. "You. Aren't you one of those Morgan boys? You must be the bad one."

"I probably am, ma'am."

"Of course you are. If you were the good one, you'd be wearing a suit and tie."

"I probably would, ma'am." He looked around at the rest of the guests, who, like him, were dressed casually in Crocket County High spirit wear and jeans. A few wore khakis and golf shirts, but most everyone else dressed down. Way down. Brandon probably *would* wear a tie to this and not look out of place.

They bid good-bye to Mrs. Hatchet, and Justin nodded

to someone across the room who waved at him. "Who's that?" he asked Allie and caught her scent. Again. Why had she put that perfume on from the other night for this? It wasn't a fancy party. He didn't need to smell how sexy she was, to remember her pressed up against him—

"Eric Washburn."

"No shit?" He tried not to stare. He saw a little of his old friend in the overweight, bald man in the stretched-tight T-shirt, but it was a challenge.

She put her hand on his arm, slender fingers cool against his too-tight skin. "Why don't you go say hello? I'm going to look and see if anyone's bid on our basket yet."

"Okay." He found himself reluctant to leave her side. He wasn't sure he knew how to behave in a real social situation. The anniversary party hadn't worked out so well. He'd gotten drunk, molested his best friend's little sister, and ended up on crutches. Of course, here he was, fantasizing about putting that same little sister in jeopardy again. Not that he was behaving any more gentlemanly on the living room couch, in the rickhouse— "Yeah, I should go." Far away, where she wouldn't have to be around him and his negative energy.

"Go on, I'll catch up with you in a minute. Just be careful of that shoulder. We don't have time to get it replaced before we leave for Georgia." She grinned and shooed him off, then walked away, leaving him alone in the big gymnasium without an anchor. It had been so long since he'd seen his high school friends, football teammates, he didn't know what he'd say to anyone but Allie.

She approached the row of tables against the wall, smiling and chatting at a very tanned brunette with, he figured, very fake breasts. Allie's natural, medium-sized curves and creamy skin were about a million times more attractive.

He could remind himself as often as he wanted that she was off-limits, but the way she looked at him…touched him…kissed him… What would she do if he were to grab her by the hand and drag her out of a side door? Push her back against the wall behind the gym and reach—

She looked over her shoulder at him and smiled.

"Hey, buddy, are you going to stand here and ogle your date all night, or are you going to come share some Blue Mountain goodness with your homeys?"

Saved by his former center, Kyle Cooper.

Shaking off the fantasy, he said, "No bourbon tonight. I've got something even better." He held up the bag containing a few jars of Rainbow Dog and the ice was broken enough for him to slip through.

• • •

"I can't believe you finally got Justin Morgan to go on a date with you." Bailey Walsh scratched through the eleventeen layers of product on her hair with a deadly fingernail. What was that, Kevlar?

"It's not really a date," Allie felt obligated to explain. "He's hurt, and the rest of the families are off on a cruise, so I'm helping him this week. And we're working on a new product project together. We're just friends."

Bailey waited for her to finish her litany and then said, "Well, the way he was staring at your booty just now, you'd better reconsider trading up to 'friends with benefits.'"

Allie whipped her head around just in time to see Justin limp across the room with a giant bald man, who had taken possession of him and was poking through Justin's bag of Rainbow Dog samples.

Bailey laughed. "Give it up. You haven't gotten over him. I'm impressed you brought him here, knowing half of our classmates are going to tease you about how you thought he was so in love with you before he ditched you for Merilee."

Allie stared.

"You didn't think we knew?"

"I'd hoped." She'd really thought since no one but Merilee and Eve had witnessed her humiliation, that no one else knew about it.

"Well, when you bragged about him coming home to see you, and then we saw Merilee groping him all over Crockett County for two weeks…and you were MIA until we all went off to college…yeah. It was pretty obvious."

The old hurt came back full force. Not just that Justin hadn't really been in love with her, like she'd convinced herself, but that everyone knew what an idiot she'd been.

No wonder her own family wouldn't give her any responsibility at the distillery. They could probably see some sort of glaring defect of judgment she wasn't aware of yet. Her Rainbow Dog project was doomed to fail.

From across the room, Justin turned to look at her. His brow furrowed, and he tilted his head in her direction, a silent, "Are you okay?"

Thinking of all that was at stake, and that there was no backing out now, she forced a smile and gave him a thumbs-up. He returned her smile, the full-on Justin-powered one that had told her first-grade self she would sell that last pitcher of lemonade to the next tractor that came around the bend. She turned back to Bailey, and said, "Did you see our new project?"

. . .

Justin had no idea what had Allie looking so sad, and he was tempted to crutch his way back across the gym and follow through with his plan to drag her outside. He wanted to run his hands through that reddish blondish—whatever color it was—hair, until she told him what was wrong.

Being among all of their classmates made Dave's absence that much sharper; maybe it did for her, too. But all he knew to do from across the gym was to grin and bear it. Then she smiled and appeared to snap out of it.

If only the Crockett County offensive line alumni would drop the subject.

"Remember when Dave McGrath told that defensive end from Gallatin County that he smelled like the underside of a quarantined bull with an erection lasting longer than four hours?"

"Oh, fuck. And the guy was like, 'No I don't,' and Dave went, 'I knew you'd know what that smells like.'"

"Damn. I wish he was here, don't you?"

Justin responded with an adept subject change. "There are a lot of people who aren't here. Where's your sister?"

He addressed Will Cooper, the younger brother of a girl he'd dated off and on, Merilee.

"She hit the big time, dude. Married a guy from Scotland with a shit-ton of money. Venture capitalist. He died a few months ago—skydiving accident—and she took over the business. Holy fuck. She's doubled the fifteen jillion dollars he left her."

"No shit."

"Really. You should look her up."

Justin thought about Merilee. They'd had a lot of fun together, did the whole high-school-sweetheart thing for a while, but at the core of things, neither of them was head over heels for the other, something they'd agreed about over drinks a few years ago. They'd drifted apart while he was in the service, and he really hadn't missed her.

But now she was a venture capitalist? How about that. He happened to know someone who needed an investor.

"You know, man, maybe I will give her a call. You got her number?"

"Yeah, you got any more of that Blue Dog shit?"

The conversation went downhill from there, when someone had to start talking about how his kid's crap turned bright green every time he drank red Kool-Aid. But the good news was that even the microbrew snobs had given Allie's Rainbow Dog flavors a taste and didn't turn their noses up too far.

. . .

Every time Allie looked across the room, Justin was talking to someone else, laughing, greeting men he knew either with the soul clasp, pull and thump bro hug, or a good-old-boy shake and back slap. Meanwhile, Allie had had at least eight different new varieties of perfume transferred to her during the "Omigod-I-can't-believe-how-good-you-look!" girl greeting.

Allie had kept in Facebook- or Snapchat-touch with most of her friends from high school, but many of them had moved away, starting families and/or careers in other parts of the country, and this was the first time she'd seen them in years.

She'd been teased about being born with a charred oak spoon in her mouth—made from the most select bourbon barrel, of course—but she was suddenly very aware that she was nowhere near as far along in life or a career as her friends. She spent the next hour fielding questions.

"Any kids?"

She imagined a little boy, with her red hair and Justin's carefree smile, charming her out of scolding him for pulling his sister's hair. A little girl, chubby-cheeked and sturdy, wrapping her daddy around her little finger.

"Are you married?"

Allie looked at Justin, imagining him in a tux. Maybe a tacky blue one with a ruffled shirt. She giggled. He would so totally rock that look.

"Engaged?"

She thought about riding a Ferris wheel, getting stuck at the top and being surprised with a diamond solitaire, kissing in the sky...

"Living with anyone?"

Coming in the door after a long day of selling Rainbow Dog, her studmuffin former marine boyfriend greeting her with his jeans unbuttoned and barely covering his hips, holding a spatula. She'd drop to her knees...

"At least dating someone special?"

"Nope."

Justin shot her a glance from across the room. It was almost like he needed to check and make sure she hadn't left him there. Which was ridiculous, because if anyone was the social center of the universe, it was Justin Morgan.

But there was more than just her relationship status to consider.

Too many people had asked variations of, "What are you doing these days? Don't all you McGraths and Morgans get to be a vice president of something when you reach a certain age?"

Allie handed out shots of Rainbow Dog to everyone she saw, thinking about making a drinking game for herself out of it: every time someone told her about their own job, she'd take a hit of Blue Dog. About their kids, Red Dog. Their husband's job…she'd be praying to the porcelain god before the raffle winners were announced.

Mercifully, the squeal of microphone feedback announced, "Everyone, listen up!" The ancient athletic director growled, "Thanks for coming out. Let's get started with the Rockett fight song as we find our seats."

As Mr. Perry's two-pack-a-day, off-key rendition of "Light 'em up Rocketts" began, Allie felt a shiver run down her spine.

"Do we have to stay for all the rest of this shit?" Justin rumbled into her ear.

Turning, she saw that even though he still wore that famous Morgan smile, faint white lines radiated from his eyes, and a muscle in his jaw twitched.

"What's wrong? Is your leg bothering you?"

"Yeah, that's it."

"Okay…" She dug the car keys from her bag as they made their way to the exit, saying good-bye to a few people on the way out. "I'll get the car."

"That's okay." He crutched right along with her.

"I thought your leg's bothering you."

He shrugged then admitted, "I really just need a break from the noise and shit. All those people wanting to talk about what it was like, did I kill anyone over there…"

"Seriously? People ask that?"

"You'd be surprised."

Allie looked over her shoulder at the building they'd spent so many important years in. "No, not really."

They reached his mom's SUV, where his leg fit best, and she unlocked the door, taking his crutches and tossing them in the back as he folded himself into the seat.

Getting into the driver seat, she noticed how comfortable she was with Justin tonight. And how amazing he smelled, shut in the car with her. Much better than the Macy's perfume counter she had rubbed all over her shoulder. "Hang on." She pulled off her own long-sleeved Rocketts T-shirt and tossed it in the backseat. Then, wearing just a camisole and bra, shoved the keys in the ignition.

"Wow. I didn't realize we'd progressed this far in our relationship. But really, Sneezy—don't you think you should at least pull around behind the building before you get nekkid?"

She reached back and retrieved the shirt, holding it to his face.

He inhaled and sneezed.

"Ha! Who's Sneezy now? They really should have a class called 'Less Is More' as a graduation requirement for Crockett County. I smell like that from getting hugged."

"Ugh. Glad I stayed on the boys' side of the gym, no matter how much I hated the schmoozing."

When she started the car, she said, "Actually, *you* rescued *me*. If I had to hear, one more time, how successful everyone else is at being an adult, I might toss up all those crab thingies I ate."

"That sucks. Who said you're not successful?" He appeared genuinely puzzled.

"No one said it. I *know* it."

As she reached for the gearshift, Justin put his hand over hers.

"Allie, I don't know dick about success. But I do know that whatever it is, if you want it, you're going to get it. If anyone has the balls to pull off this Rainbow Dog thing, it's you."

His gaze shone with sincerity, and her eyes suddenly filled.

Nodding, she covered her mouth and uttered a muffled "thanks" before faking her own sneeze and throwing the shirt in the backseat again. "Let's get home. We need to get an early start tomorrow, and I need to iron my dress."

"Huh?"

"Didn't I tell you? We're going to Keeneland. To a bachelorette party. For my college roommate."

"Oh, goody."

Chapter Ten

"Allie!" the woman shrieked toward Allie and Justin through the morning dew, high heels sinking into the damp grass outside Keeneland, center of the Thoroughbred racing universe. Even the parking area was cushy.

Enormous coils of blond hair, topped by a miniature crown with filmy veil stuff attached, bounced and shook as Allie's friend clutched her in long, skeletal arms. Justin stood out of the way, lest he suffer hair-spray poisoning. Besides, someone had to be alive to call the EMT squad if Allie choked on whatever it was that made hair do…that.

"Oh, Gabrielle, it's soooo good to see you," Allie squealed, jumping up and down, obviously as glad to see her friend as Gabrielle was to see her. She caught Justin watching her, and her hopping and jiggling became more of a smooth, but less interesting, hug.

Three other women approached more sedately — another blonde nearly identical to Gabrielle, except with a harder look to her and significantly more tanning bed points. She faked a smile at Allie but gave him a warmer look.

The other two women were brunette, one tall and curvy, the other short and slender.

"Gabrielle, I'd like you to meet my...family friend, Justin Morgan," Allie said, pulling the bride-to-be closer.

He nodded and reached out a hand. Gabrielle took it, her grip firm and friendly. "It's nice to meet you."

"Yeah, hi, Justin." The hard-eyed blonde had reached them. She licked her lips as she smiled at him.

"This is Jessica," Allie said. "She's a stripper."

He nearly choked on his coffee.

"I'm a *dancer*," Jessica corrected, her smile never wavering. "I don't take off my clothes. In public." She added, "I was classically trained and spent a few years in New York, but moved home to care for my mother, who's ill. I dance at a cabaret in Cincinnati a couple of nights a week to stay in shape."

"How, uh, nice," Justin said.

"And this is Emily." Allie drew the tall girl forward, "And Karen." The smaller woman nodded at him and gave him a little wave, followed by a look at Allie that Justin might have interpreted as approval, if he were looking for such a thing. Which he wasn't. Because, he reminded himself, he wasn't thinking of Allie that way.

He promptly forgot everyone's name, except the stripper, because she had "Jessica" emblazoned in questionably tasteful rhinestones across her generous bosom.

"It's so nice of you to do this for me," the bride told Allie as the group made its way toward the camper. Allie had set it up with the awning extended and a couple of little tables and chairs next to it.

"When you told me you were having a bachelorette party, I thought this would be a perfect opportunity to practice our bartending skills with a little tailgate party."

How in the hell had he gone from rising with the dawn to trudge through dust and heat, all the while trying to keep himself and his comrades alive, to playing bartender at a bachelorette party? The sense of disconnect was so complete that he felt like he was operating in an alternate universe.

Justin forced himself back into his own body, put his coffee on the table he was using as a bar, and opened a cooler while Allie handed out pint-size mason jars she'd decorated with bride-y crap: white ribbons and flowers and lacy shit and discreet little labels that said "Rainbow Dog, Blue Mountain." She'd told him that if things worked out, they could get jars engraved with a logo. *Faboo*, Justin thought, rolling his eyes—though he secretly thought that would be cool.

"I'm working on some cute little dog labels. I just don't have them from the printer yet."

Justin had no idea when she'd done this. He'd assume she didn't sleep, except he'd seen her last night, sacked out, when he got up to get a glass of milk. She was on the couch, arms and legs splayed, blanket on the floor. Not a care in the world. Apparently not even cold in the tiny tank top and shorts she wore. Until he covered her with the quilt and sneaked back to bed, feeling dirty—and aroused.

The women cooed and purred over the decorations while Justin poured drinks one-handed, holding himself upright— barely—with one crutch. After being on his feet for so long at last night's alumni fund-raiser, his leg was stiff and his side was sore—but he wasn't going to tell Allie that. She'd try to make him go inside the camper and lie down, and he wasn't about to miss whatever was going to happen today. He had to admit, since she'd come up with this harebrained scheme to be a moonshine mogul, his life had gotten significantly more interesting. Today's dry run with the camper was going smoothly so far, but you never knew.

Besides, he sensed that she needed his help with the toxic Jessica. Who was leaning against the table, watching him pour drinks as Allie and Gabrielle greeted another handful of squealing college friends.

"So. You're the soldier," Jessica said.

"I was. A marine."

"What are you doing now?" she asked.

"Quality assurance for the family business."

"So you drink bourbon." She raised a well-arched eyebrow.

"I drink bourbon," he agreed.

"Allie was always so cute in college—she had your picture on her bulletin board."

"Yeah?" Justin was curious in spite of himself.

"She wouldn't tell us anything about you, though. Just that you were some guy she knew from home."

He shrugged. "I guess that's what I was. Am."

"I don't know," Jessica said. "I caught her crying one time when she was drunk, holding your picture. She just said she was worried about you and her brother.

"Huh," he said, keeping his response noncommittal, but something around his diaphragm gave a thump. Jessica continued, "Any-hoo, she didn't let that stop her from sampling every guy on campus."

He handed Jessica a cocktail. Maybe filling her mouth with Rainbow Dog would keep her from spewing so much crap. He really didn't need to hear about Allie sleeping with anyone else. Errr…anyone at all, that was, because she wasn't going to be sleeping with him, either.

"Will you join me?" she held up her glass.

"No, it's a little early for me. Someone's got to remember to herd everyone toward the racetrack after a bit."

"Are you going to let me choose a horse for you?"

Jesus. This woman didn't stop. Allie shot them a glance as though she knew Jessica was talking about her, and then turned away. Jessica the Dancer-Not-a-Stripper was a friend, at least of the guest of honor, and everyone was a potential Blue Mountain customer—that had been ingrained in the Morgan boys from the time they could talk. *You're representing the family business every time you leave this house*, his father would say. But this potential customer seemed to have it in for his partner, and he was going to keep her from getting in any more digs at Allie. He supposed his mission to look out for her by helping her get Rainbow Dog off the ground should involve distracting mean girls.

Which meant he was going to have to keep Jessica busy. Grabbing a bag of lemons from the cooler, he said, "Hey, how are you with a knife and a cutting board?" He wasn't too sure that giving this piece of work a knife was a good idea, but he had to try.

• • •

By the time Allie got the bridal party to the front gate of the track, she was ready to quit.

Justin and Jessica were in front of her, their heads bent together over the racing form.

She couldn't believe it. He was picking up a...stripper... client...bitchface frenemy right in front of her! Granted, she didn't have any dibs on him. But it was unprofessional. That's what it was. She'd talk to him about it later. In a professional manner.

Thank God, the bugle signaling the start of the first race sounded.

"Oh, no!" Jessica pouted. The Bitch. "I wanted to bet on Justin's Pride. I bet he's quite the stallion."

"You know it, babe," Justin said, winking at her.

Allie rolled her eyes. "Well, you can put it all on Bimbo's Humiliation, instead."

Justin shot her a look that said, "Take it down a notch," but she ignored him.

"I didn't see that one. Which race is that in?" Jessica scanned the racing form.

He started to laugh, but quickly recovered when the bimbo in question—who had been born and raised in Lexington, Kentucky, and therefore should have learned to understand betting on horses in first grade—turned back to him, asking something inane about odds and reading the racing form.

"Allie, I really want to thank you for putting this together," Gabrielle said. "Are you sure you won't stay and play the ponies with us? We're getting a limo to drive us to dinner and clubbing afterward."

"No, thanks, G. I appreciate the invite, but I've got to get ready to head out on a business trip."

"Oh, right," Gabrielle said, winking. She leaned forward

to whisper in Allie's ear, "He can't keep his eyes off you."

Allie laughed, hoping it sounded realistic. "Like you'd keep your eye on the mean dog next door, ready to run as soon as it makes a move!"

"I'm serious!" Gabrielle protested.

After exacting a promise to send photos from the destination wedding being held in Saint Lucia, Allie waved her off.

"I'm sorry you're not coming in with us," Jessica was saying to Justin. She left her hand on his arm until he pulled it away. She handed Justin a business card that he looked at, then tucked into his back pocket. "Thanks, babe," he said.

Allie felt a little sick.

Turning to her, Jessica said, "I sure hope you find someone who suits you soon." She made a fake sympathetic face. "It's nice that your old crush steps up to be your escort when you need it, though."

Justin cleared his throat. "Baby, we've got to get going," he said, moving toward Allie for the first time that day. He put his arm around her and tugged her close to his side.

If he'd dropped on one knee and whipped out a ring she couldn't have been more surprised. The kiss he pressed to her temple nearly dropped her.

Jessica's mouth fell open. "I thought you said there was nothing between the two of you," she said.

Allie looked up at him, waiting, one eyebrow raised. The other one was paralyzed from the kiss he'd landed next to it.

"Did I say that? You must have misinterpreted my words. There *was* nothing between us. You know, back then. There's a whole lot between us now." He gave her a squeeze that nearly popped Allie's lungs. "Right, puddin'?"

"Oh, there's all kinds of stuff between us right now,"

she agreed. And it was getting deeper and smellier by the moment.

As the bachelorette crew made its way into the grand-stand, Allie turned to Justin and said, "Puddin'?"

He shrugged. "I was working on the fly. I'm not as quick on my feet as I used to be."

"What the hell was that all about? I thought you were going to go in the camper with her and put the Do Not Disturb sign out, and then all of a sudden I'm *Puddin'*?"

They had reached the camper, so she gently pushed Justin toward a chair to sit for a while so she could clean up. "Rest your leg and those ribs."

"She seems to have it in for you. I figured it was my job as vice president of schmoozing to keep her out of your hair."

Allie stopped with a handful of paper plates and stared at him.

He leaned back in the folding chair, looking as relaxed as any other race fan, running a hand through his jumbled mess of hair, then stretching his massive shoulders. She appraised him, lounging with one long leg splayed, the other propped on a cooler. The golden brown hairs on his good leg glinted in the early-afternoon sun. The strong bones and muscles forming his knee invited her to move toward him, to trace his kneecap, to follow those thigh muscles under the leg of his baggy cargo shorts… God, he was beautiful. And she knew she could count on him. He actually believed in her—the one person besides her siblings who had ever thought she could do anything. And the only one who was here helping her now.

"Thanks."

His blue eyes met hers, held. "You're welcome."

• • •

Justin's voicemail message notification chimed just as he
leaned back against the headrest in the copilot's seat of the
camper. Allie maneuvered the Suburban Assault Vehicle,
as they'd dubbed the old motor home, out of the racetrack
grounds and pointed it toward home.

He ignored the message. He couldn't think of anything
that was important enough to distract him from watching
Allie drive like the happy camper she was. Her eyes shone,
and strands of that crazy red-blond hair flew around, sliding
against her sun-kissed skin in the breeze from the open
window. Her energy was infectious as she chattered about
what people had said and new ideas she had.

It had been a successful event, and several of the par-
tygoers, as well as a few people who were tailgating nearby,
had asked for information about Rainbow Dog.

She'd graciously lied through her pearly white teeth and
told everyone that it would be available at their local liquor
stores within the next couple of months, and if they didn't
see it, to be sure and ask about it.

Justin didn't really register what she was saying, though.
He was distracted by the slender muscles in her arms as she
turned the steering wheel of the camper, the curve and slight
bounce of breast when they hit a bump. Her loose, flowing
skirt rose a few inches every now and then, exposing those
amazing thighs. He clenched his hands on his armrests to
avoid reaching over to trace the hemline over her nearest
leg. Was she ticklish?

Asshole. Touch her while she's driving so she can jerk her leg off the brake when she needs it, wreck the camper, and die. Since burning the damned rickhouse down around her didn't work.

Reason number nine thousand and six why he couldn't touch Allie McGrath.

He pulled out his phone and looked at the caller ID. Oh, shit. Merilee had returned his call and left a message. He pressed the phone against his right ear, hoping the music from the radio was loud enough to cover anything the message said. "Hi, Justin! Great to hear from you. I'm interested to hear what you have in mind. Call when you can."

He would. As soon as possible.

Allie parked the camper in the lot behind the Blue Mountain offices, and Justin slowly straightened his leg. He could bend it enough to ride, but changing the angle was a slow process after he'd been sitting for a while.

"Hey, how are your ribs?" Allie asked, opening the door to the camper to get to the cooler full of leftovers.

"Fine," he said.

"Really."

"Yes, really," he lied. He hoped she didn't feel the need to—

"Let me see the bruise," she said, ignoring the cooler and coming to him to lift his shirt.

He batted at her hands—when he really would have preferred pulling them to him. "It's fine."

"Then let me see."

"You just want to perv on my abs," he said, trying to keep things light, to deflect how badly he craved her touch.

"Well, yeah. And to check your manscaping."

"I don't have any more or less chest hair than I had yesterday," he told her.

Her hands warmed his skin as she pressed against his side. The heat traveled along his abdomen, lower, making his shorts tight.

"I guess you're going to live."

He wasn't so sure. "Is this your old-time 'laying on of hands' healing ceremony?" Her hair smelled of fresh grass and sunshine, and that damned perfume.

"Only with whiskey instead of rum." Her face was turned up to him, lips slightly parted. She'd gotten a little sun, and her freckles were popping.

He wondered which flavor of Rainbow Dog she'd taste like today. He cleared his throat and stepped out of the danger zone. As much as he'd like to lose himself in her, he couldn't.

They came from the same world, but his had become so different when he'd gone to war. He had nothing in common with her friends, to whom everything was both so temporary and earth-shattering at the same time. He'd turned himself into someone who focused on getting from one day to the next, through each deployment intact.

After Dave died, he found sanctuary in that single-minded survival plan. He hid in the Marine Corps until he couldn't hide anymore. They said the war was over, so he got out when his enlistment was over. And now he was here, trying to relate to bridesmaids.

"I was thinking. Maybe *you* could be the face—or rather, the body—of Rainbow Dog."

Justin groaned. "I don't think so. I plan to gain fifty pounds in the next several months."

"Oh, come on! Why not?"

"Why not? Because it's— I'm just not going to do that." He snorted, picturing himself romping across the pages of an ad in *Men's Fitness* with polo ponies, carrying a jar of Rainbow Dog.

"You're the perfect spokesmodel. You're young, attractive, affluent—"

"Affluent in the 'you haven't a cent to your name' way." At least not without selling his soul to his father.

She waved that off. "We'll get rich with Rainbow Dog. You'll see." She hoisted one end of the cooler while he took the other with a crutch-free arm. They chucked it onto the back of the golf cart.

"I'm not going to be a spokesmodel."

"You kinda already are," she said.

"I'm your bartender and can carry on a conversation with strangers."

"And keep strippers too busy to torment nice girls." She lifted one eyebrow.

"I have many, many skills that you haven't seen." Nor would she, he reminded himself.

It was her turn to snort. "Fine. Let's go take this leftover food to Caleb and Sherry at the distillery. See if they want to have dinner with us."

"Okay." Good. Caleb and Sherry could be chaperones for a few hours, before Justin had to trot his willpower back out.

Chapter Eleven

As they made their way across the gravel parking area away from Caleb and Sherry's little house, Allie noticed that Justin was actually moving faster on his crutches than she was in her sneakers.

He called, "Hey! Get a move on, Sneezy. It's been a long day and I'm still convalescing."

"I'm coming." The nickname rankled her, as usual. The only time he called her Allie was when... When was the last time he'd called her by her name? The other day on the couch, maybe. Heat pooled low in her belly when she thought of how he'd felt over her, in her hand.

Justin wouldn't consider her for any kind of a relationship—she understood now that he wasn't built for that. Why then did she still want him so fiercely—maybe even more so than when she was so much younger? It was probably because she knew what sex was all about now and could imagine what it would be like with him. Even if it were just a casual hookup, it would be mind-blowing.

Except it wasn't going to happen.

She took a cleansing breath. Okay. Time to get over it. Move on. He was determined that she was "Sneezy," kid sister of his best bud. Not someone he should have a sexual interest in. Stupid, honorable man.

Justin leaned on his crutches next to the tailgate of her truck, staring up at the new moon in the clear black night. He sighed.

She came to a stop nearby and breathed in the familiar aromas of Blue Mountain—fermented corn, bourbon—and Justin. His big body gave off so much heat he was like a beacon to her on the chilly April night. She forced herself to stand her ground and not move any closer.

"I wonder what the sky looks like out West," he said, not looking at her.

"Where you're going? Probably pretty hazy with all that smoke."

He chuckled, the sound a low huff. "Hopefully not all the time."

"Are you sure that's what you want to do? Go out there and jump out of perfectly good airplanes into burning trees? It's not like jumping out of perfectly good trees into burning bushes worked out so well for you."

He chuckled. "We were trying to swing over the bush. It's not my fault the Tarzan vine wasn't strong enough."

"Maybe you should have tried going one at a time," she said, thinking about the time he and Dave started a fire in a dead bush, and then tried to swing over it, re-creating some comic-book-hero story. They failed. Fortunately, the burns were only second degree. The grounding and week spent cleaning out fireplaces at the nearby state park was more painful, if Allie remembered correctly.

"Anyway," she said, unwilling to let it go this time. "Why are you leaving?"

"I don't belong here. I never have." He held up a hand to ward off her protest. "Not with our families. At the distillery. Maybe it's because Brandon and Dave were such naturals. Tasting, marketing, logistics… My skill set is pretty limited to consumption."

"You don't have to move all the way to Bum Fuck—where, Idaho? Montana? To get away from the distillery, if you hate it that much."

He didn't answer for a long minute. But as he turned toward the passenger door of Allie's pickup truck, she thought she heard him mutter something that sounded an awful lot like, "I'm worried that I don't hate it as much as I thought, 'cause I've still got to go."

They rode up the hill to the log house silently. Allie unlocked the door and held it open for him. She said, "If you're okay, I think I'll stay at my house tonight. You seem to be getting around pretty well now."

He tilted his head at her, as though he didn't understand the words, then said, "Actually, I'm pretty sore. Between the ribs and my leg, I was hoping to take a pain pill and soak in the tub for a while—I'm not sure…" He rubbed his side, the hem of his shirt riding up enough to display those abs she teased him about earlier.

Maybe she could run home and get some lingerie to

scrub on that washboard. What she said was, "You shouldn't do that when you're home alone."

He smiled at her, hopeful puppy, waiting for a treat, all over his face.

Naturally, the moment she realized she needed to get some distance, he'd get needy.

"Do you mind?"

"Of course not. I just thought you'd, you know, like some privacy." She'd actually been trying to let him go a little bit. But she was his friend. And she'd agreed to help him, right?

Oh, who was she kidding? Deciding to stick to the "friend" flight plan hadn't magically removed her desire to be around him as much as she could. She'd keep her hands to herself, but she was still going to be a little human satellite, orbiting planet Justin and his extra-gravity stomach muscles.

He looked pleased at her acquiescence and smiled as he pushed the door shut behind her, using a crutch as an arm extension.

"You know," she said, "you can't take those pills if you've been drinking. Maybe you should stick to Advil."

He hesitated for an instant, then said, "I'm sober."

He was right, as far as she knew. And she'd been with him pretty much constantly since Dave's birthday. Even when they'd been at that alumni party last night, she didn't think he'd had anything to drink.

He may not have been drinking, but dark circles under his eyes showed long nights spent doing something other than sleeping.

"Are you resting okay at night?" she finally asked.

He shrugged. "I nap." And that was all he had to say about that. He pushed past her and *thunk*ed down the hall,

Allie trailing in his wake.

Maybe if she was patient, and didn't scare him to death with her lust vibes, he'd open up to her some more.

The bourbon was being left on the shelf—because he was too distracted to drink? Maybe if she kept him busy enough, he'd be too exhausted to stay up all night thinking troubled thoughts.

He was halfway down the hall before she moved to follow him. Dang, those cargo shorts looked *good* on his butt. But then, she liked him in jeans and dress pants, too. And without. She shook her head. She was here to be a friend. Friends don't mentally undress friends.

"If you're just going to soak, do you want to use the hot tub on the back deck?" she asked. That would be good. She wouldn't have to be up close and personal with his naked body in the bathroom if he got in the hot tub.

He turned his head and said, over his shoulder, "Yeah, I guess so. You gonna get in with me?"

• • •

Justin knew that asking Allie to get in the hot tub with him was pushing it. But when she said she was thinking of sleeping at home, he felt…bereft or some pansy-assed thing like that. They'd had such a great day he wanted to prolong it. And he was sober. He could keep his hands to himself.

The idea of soaking in hot water, under the frosty sky, chatting with her a little more, making her laugh, letting her make him laugh…well, he didn't deserve it, but he wanted it. And she *did* deserve it. If hanging out with him could be considered a good thing.

"I don't have a suit here with me, and I'm not getting naked on your back porch," she told him.

He noticed that she didn't say, "I'm not getting naked with you," but he shoved that out of his mind. While he might have admitted to himself that he wanted her around, he still wasn't going to be an asshole and sleep with her. Dave's ghost would float over to the New Orleans section of heaven and pick up a zombie potion and use it on himself. Then Zombie Dave would rise from Arlington and find the motor home, whenever they were at the most remote camping spot of their trip, and open up a can of whoop-ass never before seen by man.

"Just wear one of those tank top things and shorts," he said. "I'd tell you to go through Mom's stuff and borrow one of her suits, but I think she took them all on the cruise with her. She said something about not being able to decide."

Mostly, the thought of Allie in one of his mother's modest one-piece swimsuits with the little skirty thing kind of skeeved him out.

And then it made him wonder what she'd look like when she was old enough for grandchildren, laughing as she chased them in and out of the surf on a beach vacation.

Sheesh.

She thought a minute, but he'd apparently shot down her arguments pretty well, because she finally said, "Okay, I guess. It *would* feel good to float around a little."

A few minutes later, when he came out of the bathroom, she was in his room, and he wasn't so sure this had been a good idea at all. She was bent over in booty shorts that said "Kiss it" across the ass, digging in his bottom dresser drawer. She finally came up with board shorts he was pretty sure he'd had since middle school.

"I'll just wear some gym shorts." Maybe not a great idea. Wet knit was going to show her just how much being near her affected him. Though she already knew that. But it was dark out. And hell, she'd already seen him in less.

"I can't believe you don't own a swimsuit," she said, turning.

His heart stuttered and his dick twitched. She didn't have on a tank top. She had on a sports bra. At least it was black, not white. If he'd been able to see the dark circles of her nipples, he'd have had a heart attack and would end up with an erection lasting more than four hours.

Her hair was up in some sort of complicated twisty arrangement that had probably taken about thirteen seconds to put together, held with one chopstick. What was up with that? If she was going for the "hardly any makeup and a ponytail" look, it would have taken her three hours. At least, that was the way it had worked for the occasional girlfriend he'd hooked up with over the past few years.

In Justin's experience, the lower-maintenance a woman appeared to be from the outset, the higher the price in the long run. He'd finally opted for the "What was your name again?" option when it came to girlfriends.

Allie, though, didn't fit in any of those categories. He already knew who she was. She was a little bit of everything.

* * *

Hot water enveloped Allie's legs and hips, pulling her down into chlorine-scented comfort. Justin leaned against the far side of the hot tub, his muscle-laden arms stretched along the edge, water licking at the dark hair on his chest, flirting with his nipples. This was a bad idea.

He stared at her through heavy-lidded eyes. Oh, shit, maybe this really *was* a bad idea.

"Did you already take that pain pill?" she asked. There was a warning, right there on the side of the hot tub, which said not to get in if you were under the influence of drugs or alcohol.

"Nope. I'm saving it until I'm horizontal," Justin said, bending his head this way and that, stretching his neck.

Satisfied he wasn't going to suddenly pass out and fall under the surface, Allie gingerly sat on the molded seat on her side of the tub. She'd mentally drawn a line she wouldn't cross, no matter how much her libido and his bedroom eyes tried to convince her otherwise. She'd put Justin in the friend zone, and she wasn't going to violate that rule the first night of the new season.

She sank down until the water reached her collarbone and sighed. Was there anything as glorious as hot water on a chilly night? The stars winked at a few planes making their way across the sky.

For a while, the only sound was the hot tub's motor, gently churning the water. She sneaked a peek at Justin and caught him watching her again. Her already-warm skin grew hotter. She should wish he wouldn't look at her like that, but she liked it. She really liked it.

She shifted on the seat.

"Are you comfortable? Want music?" Justin reached the controls of a waterproof radio and fiddled with the buttons. Mellow jazz floated into the air.

"Really?" she said. "We must be getting old."

"Honestly, I kind of got used to the same playlist for five years, so my taste is a little rusty," Justin told her. "Feel free to choose something yourself."

She stroked closer to him, trying not to let her legs tangle with his, but helpless to avoid small brushes of her feet against his calves, the hair tickling her toes and distracting her from the numbers on the display.

The first station she landed on was a hellfire-and-brimstone preacher. She paused and turned to look at Justin. "This one might be good for you."

He splashed her in reply.

"Thank you for your input." She tried again, delicately wiping the water from her face.

The next station was playing old-time country.

"What, did they stop importing rock and roll to Kentucky while I was overseas?"

It was Allie's turn to splash Justin.

She got in one good whap at the water before he grabbed her hands to stop her.

Giggling, she tried to pull her hands free, but was laughing too hard.

When she did manage to get a hand free, he earned a major splash. This time he cursed and rose from the water slightly, grabbing her and turning her, wrapping her in his arms, hers crossed in front of her, so she couldn't lob any more water at his face.

He fell backward onto the seat. "Be careful. I'm damaged."

She snorted. "We all know that. But I think if you're going to wrestle me into submission, you don't get to play the severely-sprained-ankle card anymore."

They both must have realized the intimacy of their

positions at the same time, because the abrupt silence rang with innuendo.

Her backside was pressed against his lap, his big, muscular thighs bracketing hers, his arms holding her back against his chest. A breath skittered over her left shoulder, sending a shiver that she couldn't suppress down her spine.

The heat from his body was ten times more dangerous than the water. In spite of every resolution she'd made an hour ago, every roadblock he'd put in her path, Allie craved his embrace. Just for a few seconds. Just…just to give in and feel this, this aching want, for a brief moment in time. And then…then she could move on.

Chapter Twelve

Oh, holy hell. Justin felt Allie's sigh in her movement, the slight arch of her back, her ass nestled against his throbbing balls, his cock hard and pressed into her lower back. *Fuck.* He had to let her go before this got too intense. And he was going to. In just a second.

A drop of water fell from her hair, ran down the side of her neck, and disappeared over her shoulder. He imagined it rolling between her breasts. Somehow her head was tilted to the side, and his mouth was a hairbreadth away from her skin. He could feel the heat of her shoulder with his lips, and that elusive perfume was a taste away. It was like a magnetic force holding him there. He turned his head, ever so slightly. Surrendering, he pressed his open mouth against that spot on her neck, just under her ear.

Her sigh became a little moan when he licked her skin, salty-sweet and so smooth and tender, he thought he could probably spend the next six weeks right there, learning that small section of skin with his lips and tongue.

Her hands had come from under his hold to press his arms around her. Interlacing her fingers with his, together they explored her abdomen. He never, ever would have thought the softness surrounding a belly button would make him so fucking hard. But this was Allie's stomach.

His breath hitched; he tried not to hyperventilate, but the urge to rise onto his one good leg and turn their bodies, press her against the side of the tub, and pull those ridiculous shorts off and slide into her wet heat was consuming every synapse in his brain.

She guided his right hand higher, to the bottom of her sports bra, and hesitated. His breath froze. He couldn't let this— She pressed his hand higher until he felt the firm weight fill it, the nipple raised against the skin of his palm.

He groaned.

She gasped.

Oh, hell. He was touching her. His left hand skirted lower, just reaching the juncture of her thighs, which he had pressed tightly closed between his own. But she squirmed, and he thought maybe the very tips of his fingers were almost where she wanted them to be.

He groaned, pulling her more firmly against his groin. It wasn't enough. He was going to hell. He had a vague notion of throwing himself on the spear of the vengeful ghost of Dave McGrath, and then it was gone in a haze of lust.

She pushed away a little, and he let her go, reluctantly, knowing it was for the best, but wishing—

She turned to face him and floated back down over him, her thighs spread, straddling his lap.

One last brain cell fired, and he said, "I'm not sure this

is a good idea."

She looked at him with wide eyes and parted lips. "Life is too short to wait for good ideas."

Before he could process that concept, her mouth was on his, her tongue in his mouth, and he was licking back at her, nipping at her lips. Cherries. Today, she tasted like cherries.

She writhed against his cock, a little cry escaping as he ground back up toward her.

He slid his hands up her rib cage, cupping her breasts, squeezing, tugging at her nipples. He broke away from her mouth and bent his head, sucking one nipple into his mouth as he pulled her bra out of the way. He'd come back later and look to see if her nipple was, indeed, the same color as her lips. And then he'd see what else was that color.

Jesus, he was hard, and the wet fabric between both of them provided just enough friction that he was perilously close to coming.

But he wanted to feel her go over, to watch her, before he completely lost his mind.

He had to let go of her breasts to push her back a little, but then he slid a hand between their bodies to slip his fingers under the edge of her shorts and—oh, hell, she wasn't wearing panties under those shorts—found her, slick and swollen. He slid his fingers against her, feeling her clit twitch, trying to learn what rhythm worked for her.

She panted, little whimpers in his ear while he stroked her. She held on to his shoulder with one hand, fingernails digging into his flesh. Her other hand found his erection, caressing him. He didn't have the will to tell her to stop, even though he was fast approaching the precipice. He thrust two fingers inside her and continued to toy with her clit with his thumb.

Too quickly, she cried out and collapsed against him, throbbing around his fingers as she came.

The groan he let out a few seconds later as his own release overtook him was echoed with more pulses against his hand.

"Oh God," she said against his neck, her limbs draped around him. Reluctantly, he slid his hand from her body, but holding her against him felt pretty damn good, too. The wide-open Kentucky night above them, her arms around him, warm water below—all of his demons were far, far away tonight.

He couldn't move. Didn't ever want to. Didn't think he should. If a dry hump in the hot tub—wet hump?—left him this wrung out, actually getting inside this woman would probably kill him.

The sounds of the night, the chilly air, the smell of the bubbling water reasserted themselves, and his leg throbbed now that his blood flow was returning to normal.

Squeezing her gorgeous rump, he said, "Be my girl and move to your right an inch or so."

A sharp intake of breath, and Allie moved completely off of him.

"You don't have to go that far," he began to protest.

But she'd already scrambled out of the water, and he had to turn to see her dripping on the deck. She reached for the towels she'd put on the nearby table.

"Hey…" he started, but she shook her head.

"Let's get you out of there."

His head *thunk*ed back against the edge of the tub, and he stared up at the sky, distant, frozen stars shooting sparks of accusation at him. There were those good old demons. He'd crossed the line again—but why hadn't they reminded him to stop before he got there? He wasn't staying here, he didn't belong here, and the last person Allie needed was him. "Shit, babe. I'm sorry."

"Come on." She stood nearer now, holding his crutches and a towel, staring across the deck. Steam rose from her body, but her nipples were beaded with the cold, and she shivered.

He reached for her arm. "Hey. Look at me."

She glanced at his face, then away again.

Allie had reached something inside him, something deeper than his skin, his muscles, those nerve endings that screamed for release when she was near. He had to convince her that he wasn't going to molest her every time they were near each other—although maybe he needed to convince himself first.

"I shouldn't have touched you like that. I just—it's been a while. You know—horny guy, we're all alike." That was lame. But he didn't want her to know how much he wanted *her*. He couldn't have her. And she didn't want *him*, the guy who didn't bring her brother back from war.

She laughed, a dry, bitter sound. "Yeah. I know. I've got hormones, too, you know?"

True. She had come apart for him like nobody's business.

"Are we okay, then?" He smiled at her.

She returned it. "Of course."

He had a feeling that she wasn't any more unaffected by what had just happened than he was.

Chapter Thirteen

"That's my girl. Hope to hear from you soon." Justin's low, sexy laugh crawled like a block of ice into Allie's stomach when she walked into the Morgans' house.

Justin shoved his phone into his pocket and turned to her, surprise on his face.

She'd managed to get a good three hours of sleep before she gave up and started loading the Blue Mountain Rainbow Dog Express. Morning-after regrets had her so distracted that she'd stuffed her toiletries in the ancient, leaky-seamed backpack she'd carried in high school instead of the incredibly cool Thirty-One messenger bag Eve had given her for her last birthday. She didn't bother to rearrange, just tossed the bag into the camper along with her suitcase and came back in for—what? Now she couldn't remember.

"Hi." Her smile felt stiff, the pain and humiliation welling up in her like that long-ago day at the Lexington airport. "You ready to go?"

"Sure," he said, nothing wrong at all. No just-ended-booty-call twisting *his* conscience. No, she'd realized, staring at the ceiling last night, he might struggle with his warped sense of honor and an overactive libido in the moment, but any hurt feelings on her part belonged to her—it wasn't his fault she kept attacking him. She should know better.

As they locked up the house and finished packing the camper, she again dissected every moment of everything that had happened last night, and she was coming up with a tangle.

Their bodies couldn't seem to stay away from each other. And her heart was along for the ride. Fortunately, her brain was there to remind her that whatever happened, Justin's body was only recognizing her body. She didn't know what his heart was doing; he had that wrapped up tight and locked away.

Except she wanted him. She really, really wanted to be with him. Was she willing to take what he could give her? An orgasm now and then with no promises of more? If she really cared about him, maybe she should stay away so he didn't feel so guilty any time he succumbed to his "needs."

If only he'd stop calling her "his girl" or "babe." But there was no way she was going to explain why his generic, a-few-endearments-fit-all was an issue for her.

It was okay.

It really was. They were about to spend a week together, traveling across the heartland, promoting Rainbow Dog whiskey. It would go smoother if they maintained a professional distance. And that would happen best if they just pretended those moments in the hot tub hadn't happened.

She stashed the last case of Blue Dog into the storage

area under the camper and locked it. She said a little prayer that this trip would yield an investor for Rainbow Dog. So that she wouldn't have to see Justin give up his plans to move out West in order to stay here and repay her loan by sacrificing himself on the altar of his father's plans.

"Where's our first stop?" Justin asked.

"Nashville," she told him. "I got lucky, and there's some kind of a biker rally at the campground. I rented one of the last spots available. I figure that after we make the rounds of liquor distributors, we've got an audience with our new neighbors."

Justin groaned.

"What?" she asked him.

He was shaking his head. "Bikers? Really? Dammit, Allie, I'm kind of hobbled here."

"So?"

"So I could barely protect you from two overgrown toddlers at a playground if I had to. What am I going to do when you get up in some biker's grill, and his old lady comes after you with a knife?"

He was really worried about this. It was kind of sweet, if it wasn't so ridiculous. "I'm not going to get in trouble with bikers. I'll just offer everyone some Rainbow Dog, and see what they think of it. If they like it, they can carry the word to their respective clubs."

Justin stared at her. "Do you even *watch Sons of Anarchy*?"

Allie laughed. "These are bikers at a state park. I seriously doubt that they'll be trading guns with a South American drug cartel at The Grande Ole Opry." At least, that was her hope.

• • •

As it turned out, the bikers were scarier—to Justin, any-way—than if they'd ridden their Harleys right up to the mo-tor home and threatened to kidnap and rape the both of them at knifepoint.

They were a club of Vietnam veterans and their wives, from all branches of service, on an annual pilgrimage to Arlington to pay their respects to their fallen brethren.

He couldn't have been more uncomfortable if it had been an octogenarian pole dancers' convention. He'd man-aged to avoid Allie's attempt to get him involved in her VA volunteer activities, but had still landed in the middle of it.

Allie was out of sorts, too. "I thought this would be some kind of a badass hard-partying group," she whispered as they drove slowly through the grounds, looking for lot eighty-six. "Half of these folks look like they mix their sherry with Metamucil. They're never going to be a target audience for Rainbow Dog whiskey!"

In spite of himself, Justin laughed. "Allie, I suspect you could sell sand to the Saudis. Besides, Rainbow Dog isn't exactly a badass biker drink. It's too…colorful."

She braked and turned her head to stare at him.

"What?"

"That's the first time you've called me 'Allie,' except when—" She shook her head. "Never mind."

But he knew what she meant. He usually called her "Sneezy." Unless he'd just been kissing her. Or feeling her up. But he couldn't call her Allie all the time, because that was too close to acknowledging feelings that he wasn't going to face.

She cleared her throat. "There it is." She pointed at a sign next to the little cinder-block building that housed the men's and women's facilities.

"Nice. Right next to the bathrooms and the Dumpster," Justin said.

"Are you kidding? This is great!" she said, apparently recovered from her dismay. He had to give it to her. She didn't dwell on life's little disappointments. "Everyone's got to come by here. We'll have a chance to meet all the campers. Damn. We should have borrowed a dog from someone. Walking a dog around one of these places is another way to meet people."

"Great."

"I detect a less-than-enthusiastic tone, Justin."

"Ya think?" He didn't know how to say that he didn't want to talk to all of those veterans. They would ask him about his service. It was one thing to give bullshit all-purpose answers that people wanted to hear back home. And Allie seemed sensitive to his reluctance to talk about it all. At any rate, the few times she'd brought up Dave's name, she'd allowed him to steer the conversation to something else. These guys would see right through him.

"This will be extra nice, since they're vets. You can regale them with tales of modern warfare. You'll be the most popular kid in town."

Okay. Maybe he'd just imagined that she was sensitive to his feelings.

He sighed. "At least these guys won't ask me how many terrorists I've killed. Just pull up there." He pointed to a turnaround. "Let's unhook the car from the hitch so we can back this thing into its spot."

"Fine, Captain Cranky Pants." She drove forward a few more yards and put the camper in park, then got out to stretch.

Justin slid into the driver's seat, carefully maneuvering his bum leg around the center console. It rankled that she was going to have to do most of the physical stuff on this trip, but as he looked in the side-view mirror, he had to admit that watching her bend over to unhook the car from the hitch wasn't a terrible experience. Damn. He was having a harder and harder time—so to speak—remembering why he had to leave her alone.

He'd promised Dave he'd watch out for her. Dave hadn't said, "Don't fuck her." He'd just said to make sure she didn't get pushed aside, always the baby no one gave credit to. And to make sure people didn't take advantage of her. It wasn't that she was naive and easily conned, but she was just so damned interested in everyone that people crossed her personal boundaries without much thought. Although…if he was inside her personal boundaries himself, he could fight off marauders more easily, couldn't he?

If he wasn't careful, he'd rationalize his way into her bed. There was a big reason he wasn't going to sleep with her. She mattered to him, and she deserved better than his nasty, screwed-up self. And he needed to remember that he didn't fit into her life. He might have been sleeping a little better lately, but that was just because she was wearing him out with all of these Rainbow Dog preparations, not because he was feeling more serenity or any bullshit like that.

Allie straightened and saw him watching her in the mirror. She motioned for him to roll down the window.

"Throw me the keys!" she said.

He tossed them back to her, and she caught them in midair. "Nice throw, Peyton!"

He shook his head. She'd called him that in high school, when he'd quarterbacked the Crockett County Rocketts to the state championship. Apparently, she'd shoved him back into the friend column. Good. That was good.

After she backed the car away from the camper, Justin maneuvered the beast onto the narrow band of asphalt they'd call home for the next several days. By the time he had the thing situated, no fewer than six senior citizens with potbellies and leather vests were not-so-discreetly watching from the adjacent campsite.

Resigned to turning his man card over to the old farts next door, he let himself out of the motor home and made his way to the picnic table next to the cold fire ring.

"Afternoon." One of the old guys nodded.

"How ya doin'?" Justin sat down sideways, not wanting to be rude, but not wanting to dive into neighborliness, either.

"Where'd you serve?" asked a tall guy with a silver ponytail. The ring of men followed him onto the campsite.

Jesus. How the hell—oh. The sleeve of his T-shirt rode up due to his crutches, and his "semper fi" tattoo showed. "Afghanistan," Justin admitted. "Three tours."

"Shit, son, how long you been out?" That was from another guy with a high and tight buzz cut that had a distinct shiny patch in the highest and tightest region.

"Few weeks."

"Thanks for your service."

Justin nodded. "Same to you."

And suddenly, he was one of the guys. His new best friends all introduced themselves, and he was completely overloaded with names, branches of service, units, conflicts, and military bases. Someone offered him a beer, and after a beat, he declined. He really wanted a drink. And that alone told him how important it was that he avoid one. The last thing he needed right now was to have a buzz on while alone in a camper with Allie.

Another man, white-haired and slender, Justin thought his name was Rick, pointed at his leg and asked, "That happen to you in the line of duty?"

"Uh, no. It's more recent. I, uh, fell." He didn't know why he felt like he was losing some street cred, but he thought they'd have been more impressed if he had a Purple Heart to tell them about.

Then Allie approached with an older lady. "This is my husband, Justin," Allie said.

"Justin, this is Maureen Logankowski."

Her husband? What the fuck? She'd been out of his earshot for all of five minutes. Feeling a little nauseated, he smiled and shook Maureen's hand. She was pretty and plump, with short blond hair and tight jeans. The big guy with the ponytail said, "Hey, darlin'. You got something for me?"

Maureen smirked and said, "Yeah, but you can't have it here in front of everyone. My conJustination might have something to say about it."

Everyone laughed.

"I'm a Presbyterian minister," she told Justin.

Ah. That must be why Allie told her they were married. He hoped it was a knee-jerk panic at being in the presence of a church official, similar to being followed by a state trooper on the interstate. That sudden need to slow down and sit up straighter.

"Don't let her fool you," Ponytail Guy said. "She's still a biker's old lady."

Allie laughed, and Justin tried to join in, but when she put her arm around his shoulders and settled onto his good leg, he had a hot flash that was part panic at the thought of being married and part desire at imagining having Allie naked, any time they were both in the mood.

"Allie told me about losing her brother, your friend, overseas. I'm sorry for your loss," Maureen told Justin, laying her hand on the arm that he hadn't automatically wrapped around Allie's waist.

"Thanks," he muttered.

Allie went on to tell the men in the group about her brother David, that he'd been Justin's best friend, that their families had been in business together for generations, and served in the military when they weren't making bourbon.

She was telling the truth, and the bare minimum, but it still felt thick and heavy on Justin's soul. But maybe it was good that she told the story. Then he wouldn't have to later; no one would ask about it. The explosion, the blood, the fear…

"Hey, baby," he said, nudging her to move off his lap. "I, uh, need to go to the head." With a polite nod to the group gathered around him, he escaped.

Chapter Fourteen

Allie watched Justin disappear into the men's room, then plastered on her brightest *nothing's wrong* smile and turned back to their new neighbors. "Was there firewood for sale at the camp office? I forgot to look when we checked in." She somehow doubted she'd be able to get Justin to sit outside around the fire tonight, but she needed something to say to these people after he was so rude.

"I've got plenty. Just come over and get some—you can replace it later," said one of the men. "But we'll be having a fire over at Marty and Maureen's lot later, if you want to come."

"That's very kind. I'm not sure—we're pretty wiped out, but we may surprise you and show up."

As the men wandered back to the cooler, Maureen gave her an apologetic smile. "I'm sorry, sweetie, I wasn't thinking."

Allie sighed. "It's been two years. It was horrible. But

it happened, and sometimes Justin acts like David never existed."

"Oh, dear." Maureen leaned against the picnic table. "Marty's pretty on-the-table with his feelings, but he's got buddies who never talk about things that happened."

"And are they all still alive and functioning?" Allie had to ask.

"Some of them."

They talked for a few more minutes. Allie never had a problem talking to new people, but Maureen was exceptional—one of those insta-friends that happen now and then. After her initial panic about a minister finding out she was sleeping in the same camper with a man she wasn't married to—hence the lie—she'd started telling Maureen about feelings she hadn't even shared with Eve. New feelings, about a beautiful, bighearted—and troubled—man she was starting to know all over again—or maybe for the first time.

Maureen said good-bye, and Allie let herself into the camper. Justin sat at the little kitchen table holding an empty glass, turning it in his hands.

Determined to ignore his stay-away vibes, she opened the cabinet above the table area and got out a bottle of Blue Mountain. "Do you want a drink?" She got herself a glass and sat down opposite him.

"No." He blew out a breath. "Why did you tell them about Dave?"

She leaned back in her seat, surprised. She figured if he was going to berate her, it would be for telling everyone they were married. "It just kind of came out."

"Oh, like, 'Hi, my name is Allie, that's my fake husband, Justin, and my brother died in Afghanistan'?"

She sucked in air and let it out, slowly. It didn't help. "Yes, Justin. Exactly like that. I added a couple of shaky breaths to curry the sympathy factor." It wasn't like that at all. Maureen had told Allie that the group was headed for Arlington in a few days, and that she hoped she and Justin would stop by, too, to pay their respects to David.

"Great. Maybe you could invite a couple of those guys to chase me around and force me to tell them war stories for the next two days."

"That's a great idea!" she chirped at him, since he was determined to snarl at her.

He glared at her, eyes narrowed, jaw ticking, but then looked away. The silence in the camper threatened to suck Allie against the wall and leave her hanging there.

She opened the bottle and poured herself a shot, looking at him over the rim of the glass when she took a sip. He had dark circles under his eyes, and his complexion was sallow.

"When was the last time you got a good night's sleep?"

"Are you my mom now? Justin's grumpy, he must need a nap?"

She shrugged. "You look like you could use a test tickle."

He didn't even lip-twitch at the reference. She wasn't sure, but she thought the testicle joke had originated with David, a book about bodies, and a *Barney* episode about hugging.

"Fuck." Justin threw the empty glass across the room, where it bounced off of a cabinet and rolled harmlessly to the floor. God bless her mom and high-quality glassware, even for camping. "I haven't really slept since...since the fire."

"Are you having nightmares about it or something?"

"No, it's more like I'm not having bourbon." He looked straight at her, a challenge in his gaze.

"Do you need help? Are you having withdrawals?" Alcoholism was nothing new to Allie. Her father had been a drunk. It was a painful reality, especially in a business that fed the disease, but she and Eve had gone to Al-Anon and knew their own limits, and she wasn't afraid of booze.

"No, I'm not having fucking withdrawals or DTs or whatever. I just can't fucking sleep."

"Then have a few drinks, if it gets you through," she said, her heart aching for him, even though he was being a dick, knowing he was reacting to his own pain.

He laughed bitterly and got to his feet. Tucking his crutches under his arms, he turned toward the bedroom and said, "It's not about being an alcoholic, it's about drinking because I can't sleep at night for thinking about how hard it is to keep my fucking hands off of you."

The shock of heat that landed in Allie's belly and spread through her chest, core, and limbs had nothing to do with the liquor she'd just swallowed and everything to do with the man who disappeared with a slide of the door.

• • •

Justin was claustrophobic as hell, but the sounds of Allie banging around in the mini kitchen kept him sequestered. He would have to face her at some point. The damned bathroom was outside the bedroom door, and he couldn't piss out the window. Or could he? He sat up and pushed aside the little curtain that covered the window. It had an unremovable screen.

Nope. He'd just have to grow a pair and talk to her.

He sat up and fished around his seabag for a clean pair of cargo shorts. It was still a little chilly outside, but he was only going to sacrifice so many pairs of pants to be cut to fit over his brace, and one cold leg in shorts could survive. He stripped out of his T-shirt.

It took him five minutes and a lot of wrestling around in the tiny space, but he managed to get changed. He was refastening the brace when Allie knocked on the door. "Can I come in?"

Heart beating double time, he said, "Yeah," and watched her appear through the opening door.

"Taste this," she said, shoving a plate at him.

"Whatcha got?" His stomach growled, and he realized he hadn't eaten in a long time. He selected a cracker that had a blob of bright orange cheese in the middle. "Squeezy cheese on a saltine?"

"Sort of."

He bit down and found that, along with the canned cheese, was a tiny bite of something… "Is that bacon?"

"Yep. And a little olive slice. Now try the other one."

He took a Ritz Cracker covered with a speckled, lighter cheese, topped with a tiny pickle slice.

"That's ranch-y cream cheese."

"You're really taking some pains with your Greater Appalachian cooking," Justin observed.

"I know, isn't it great? I was thinking about putting together a Rainbow Dog cookbook. We have all this fancy stuff we troop out to go with our refined, Southern-style bourbon tastings, but that's not what Rainbow Dog is about. It's about right now, and what you've got in the pantry. No need to make a special trip out for cherrywood smoked ham and Amish goat cheese."

Justin found himself nodding. "What can you do with Velveeta?" he asked.

"Oh, baby. What *can't* I do with Velveeta?" She cocked a hip and raised an eyebrow.

A little strip of skin peeked out above the waistband of her pants, and he remembered how soft her skin was right there. He wanted to turn her around and trace the tattoo he knew would be showing while he tugged those britches down and...

He coughed and pulled on a T-shirt.

"Maureen and Marty invited us to share dinner with them. I thought I'd take these. Are you up for that?"

She'd apparently swept his earlier grenade under the rug, for which he was grateful. What he wasn't so comfortable with was the knowledge that she could pick it up and pull the pin when he was least expecting it.

Playing along, he said, "Sure." He could put on his social skills for a couple of hours. Hell, he could even wear a USMC sweatshirt. Lesser of two evils. Anything to avoid being shut in this camper with Allie any longer than he had to.

He followed her into the living area, and she asked him if he minded prepping the appetizers. "I guess so. Since I can't go outside to split wood or hunt bears, I'll be your kitchen wench."

"You've never in your life chopped wood, much less hunted anything," Allie said.

"Not true. I've even got a Boy Scout badge to prove it. The wood chopping part. I'll give you the hunting point."

The next half hour was cool, all things considered. They

brainstormed easier, more rough-around-the-edges foods that would go with flavor-boosted white dog, but thankfully quit when the ideas degenerated to chocolate-covered hash browns and lemon-vanilla hamburgers.

He almost preferred the times when he was painfully aware of how physically attracted he was to her, because this whole fun domesticity thing? It was making him think crazy shit.

Allie gathered an assortment of Rainbow Dog flavors and put them in an old-fashioned wire milk-bottle carrier. "Can you get this with your crutches?" she asked Justin, as he stood and tucked the damned things under his armpits. Just a couple more days and he'd be allowed to put weight on the foot. He was tempted to be a rebel and go early, but the thought of backsliding in his recovery and needing Allie to help him bathe for another week was too damned appealing. For the sake of sanity and world peace, he'd be medically compliant.

They strolled to Maureen and Marty's campsite on the adjacent lot, which seemed to be party central. There were at least twenty people present, gathered at the enormous grill that folded down from the back of their fifth-wheel travel trailer. Folks milled about, poking at the fire or arranging food on a couple of portable tables.

"We've brought the party," Allie said, and indicated Justin's burden. Justin handed Allie the liquor to set up on the drinks table and quirked up his mouth while he dug in the pocket of his shorts and produced a pint of Angus's Single Barrel. "Thanks for having us," he told Maureen. "I hope this is an appropriate hostess gift."

"Holy shit," the minister said. "Of course it's appropriate.

I'll be right back." She disappeared into the camper, either to stash her prize or to give it a taste.

Allie nudged him. "Well, *honey*, you sure know how to make yourself welcome."

"Yes, sweetiepoo, I do," Justin said.

"Hey, boy, get over here. Pinky here spent some time at Lejeune. He wants to bore you with his stories."

Allie had a glint in her eye that he didn't trust. He thought he saw her finger twitch on the pin of that grenade when she rose on her tiptoes to lay a big smoochy kiss on his lips. "You go on, hang with your boys. I'll be over here with the ladies, finding out which tricks will keep our marriage from going stale."

• • •

"Your man looks a lot more comfortable now," observed Maureen, handing Allie a plastic cup. The ladies had grabbed the Pink Dog and turned it into the most amazing frozen concoction. Allie had begged for the recipe, typing it into the notepad on her phone—right after asking for a refill.

Justin was splayed in a folding chair that she'd fetched for him, his head tilted back with laughter at something one of the old guys said. One of his big arms was slung over the back of the chair as he leaned toward the speaker.

"He does look pretty amazing," Allie said, then blushed.

Maureen's friend laughed. "You can say that again, sweetheart. I hear it's supposed to be warmer tomorrow. I might need you to ask him to come over and help me in the yard. He can leave his shirt in your camper."

"You did notice the bum leg, right?" Allie asked.

"He can help by providing aesthetic improvement."

All the women laughed, and the men turned to look.

"You better marry that boy for real soon," Maureen said. "He's a keeper."

Allie stared at her new friend. "I—"

"Honey, neither one of you is wearing a ring," she said.

"Oh. Well, not everyone believes in—"

A brunette with the raspy laugh of a smoker said, "Let's see. Old-school Bluegrass bourbon distillery family? I'm guessin' your ring would weigh more than you do, and you'd wear it gardening, cleaning the outhouse, and swimming in Lake Cumberland."

She was right. Even as broke as Justin was, and as unfathomable as it was that he'd ever ask his parents for money, she knew that there were diamonds in his mother's jewelry box just dying to be made into engagement rings for her sons.

"So what's the story?"

Allie had swallowed just enough of Alice's Tennessee Poodle, as they'd decided to call the frozen drink, to tell them. "I've been in love with him since I was five. Maybe longer. He barely knows I exist."

"Ha!" someone said.

"He knows you exist," another woman said. "Boy can't keep his eyes off you."

As if he knew they were talking about him, he turned his head and looked straight at Allie, unsmiling for the first time since they'd arrived.

"He might know I'm here, but he doesn't want to."

"Have you asked him?" Maureen touched Allie's shoulder.

Should she say it? "It's not about him not wanting to, uh,

you know—we've gotten pretty close a couple of times. But I think he's just horny. Which would be totally cool…" Cheeks hot, she eyed Maureen, who had nothing but understanding in her eyes. "But I'm afraid that if I push for more sexy stuff, I'm gonna get my heart broken."

The women listened quietly, then one said, "Screw that. Life is short. If you don't put your heart out there to get stomped on, you don't get nothing. You got that karaoke machine, Maureen?"

Oh, hell. This was not going to be good. "Um, I'm not sure what you've got in mind, but I don't know if I want to—"

"Yes, you do."

They were right. Her heart was already at Justin's feet. She might as well gather as many good, sexy memories as she could before he tromped all over her.

Maureen smiled, then said, "We're not going to tell our men that you're not really married. Let them torment your man a little longer with having to fake it."

Chapter Fifteen

"Oh, hell no," Marty said. The others looked around and laughed.

"What's going on?" Justin looked at the camper, and saw the minister carrying a— "Oh, hell no," he repeated.

Allie, who had wandered over a few minutes ago and sat down next to him, smiled and took a big drink of a sludgy frozen-daiquiri kind of thing.

"Honey, I think it's time for me to go to bed. You feel free to stay." He patted her on the knee, found his crutches, and started to get to his feet. "Dinner was awesome. Thanks for your hospitality."

"Oh, no, my young friend." An old marine, who'd been stationed at Camp Lejeune, put a hand on Justin's shoulder, trapping him in his seat. "If we have to sit here for karaoke time, you've got to stay, too."

Justin turned to Allie. "You're not gonna do this, are you?"

She gave him a look, narrowed her eyes. "Why? Do you

think I can't? Can *you* sing?"

He straightened, though he had a creeping suspicion his inability to back down from a challenge was about to get him in trouble. "Don't you remember that band Brandon and Dave and I had in high school? The Charred Staves?"

Allie scoffed, her sneer begging to be kissed into a laugh. "That was a death metal band. You screamed every song."

She was right. They really had sucked. He had to defend his honor, though. "And all the girls wanted to go out with me."

"Because Donna Richmond told everyone that you went dow—" Allie's hand clamped over her mouth.

Oh God. Even Allie had heard that story? "She lied. I was— I'm not quite sure how she thought that was— Anyway, I can too sing."

"I bet you I'm better."

"I bet you you're not."

"Shooee, Buddy. You just threw down one big fat hairy gauntlet, didn't you?" Marty smacked him on the back.

Allie snorted. Justin was beginning to think she might be a little drunk. He'd been so worried about keeping his own head about him, he hadn't paid much attention to her consumption. He wouldn't have thought he needed to.

"Oh, yes, you did," someone else said.

"I think he's scared." That was definitely the Camp Lejeune guy.

All of a sudden Justin felt like he was being pushed around on the playground. And as such, he was going to satisfy his inner sixth grader by rising to the challenge.

"Okay then, Mr. Drill Instructor. You first," Justin said. "Unless you're scared."

The other men hooted, but the old marine got up and

swaggered to the other side of the fire, where he conferred with Maureen for a few minutes. The other campers rearranged chairs, getting refills on drinks.

"What are the stakes?" someone asked. "You can't have a bet unless you're betting for something."

"If I win, you cut your hair," Allie said, without thinking about it. She reached out and ran her fingers through it, grazing his scalp, sending tingles along his spine, straight to his groin. "You looked so much better with your marine-guy cut—this mess looks like you're auditioning for a boy band."

Her hand froze at the back of his head, as though realizing how casually, how comfortably, she was touching him. Their eyes held. He didn't want her to stop. He wanted her to keep stroking down his shoulder, along his arm to hold his hand.

She jerked her hand away, reminding him they were talking about a bet: his hair.

He didn't want to have a fucking jarhead haircut ever again, but he was pretty sure he could win, even if he had to cheat and go for the humor vote. "Fine. And if I win, you have to make me dippy eggs for the rest of the trip."

"I hate making dippy eggs. It takes me three eggs to get one that works."

Justin just grinned at her.

"Fine." Her hands were back in her own space, waving his stakes away like it wouldn't be an issue.

"What are dippy eggs?" someone asked.

"Dippy eggs," Allie said, "are over easy for the vocabularily challenged."

"Just so you know," Justin said, "the term comes from your side of the family."

"Whatever."

The sun had slipped below the horizon a while ago, and the last pink and gold rays of the day were fading from the sky.

"Pretty sunset, huh?" Allie put her head on his shoulder. When did she get so close to him? How did his arm get draped across the back of her chair, over her shoulders, actually? "Uh-huh," he finally muttered.

She was really working the pretend-wife angle. He wondered if she was doing it to appease her sense that the minister would disapprove if they were living in sin, or if she just wanted to torment him. He was starting to think the latter. Her head turned, and she was close enough that he couldn't see her eyes clearly. Her lips were pretty well defined, though. And then her tongue came out to lick the bottom one, dragging a groan from deep within him. Without thinking about it, he leaned in for a kiss.

It wasn't a sexy kiss. It was an affectionate, I'm-glad-you're-with-me kiss, and his whole body sighed with that weird feeling he got whenever he smelled her after being away from her for a while. Peace?

A screech of feedback jolted them both. The old marine grinned, giving the microphone a couple of practice swings.

"Oh, Lord," said one of the women. "He's channeling Mick."

And sure enough, the guy went into a really, really bad rendition of "Jumping Jack Flash." It was awful, but pretty funny, because he couldn't have been less Mick Jagger had he been a four-hundred-pound woman.

Allie laughed, her shoulder under Justin's arm feeling right, and he decided, just for the next hour or so, not to get too twisted up in right or wrong or how much he was going to beat himself up later; he would just enjoy having his fake wife snuggled up against him.

A small, dark-haired woman put out her cigarette and said, "Gimme that."

She sang "Redneck Woman" almost as badly.

Someone with a little more inner tuning fork sang "Love Me Tender," and then Marty sang a surprisingly elegant Bob Dylan song.

"Okay, we've warmed up the machine and showed you ours. I think it's time for the new kids to show us theirs. Who's going first. Justin? Allie?"

Argh. Justin was rethinking that whole alcohol-free evening. He wondered if he could get Allie to go first, if he could get enough shots into himself to be able to stand up there and—

"I'll go," Allie said, turning to point a finger at Justin. "But you're going down."

"Like with that girl in high school Allie was tellin' us about?" someone called out. Justin had a feeling he was going down, but it was going to be more like a sinking ship and less like a high school kid trying to get a free anatomy lesson.

She marched to the karaoke machine with her fists clenched and back straight, a new recruit determined to pass inspection. "Just so you know, I'm only up here because my Hunk of Burnin' Love over there doesn't think I can sing. What he seems to have forgotten is that I was the Crockett County High School girls' chorus captain for two years."

"Wait," said the Redneck Woman. "I think we should get to choose the songs."

Great. Justin was really praying for the comedy vote now.

• • •

Allie watched Maureen and another woman go through the list of songs. "I think that's going to be too hard," Maureen said. "That takes a lot of range."

"You guys are making me very nervous here," Allie said. "I'm going to need another drink if we don't get this over with soon."

"She won't know that one. She's not old enough," someone else said.

Allie walked over to the screen and read the title. "I know it," she said. She wasn't quite sure it was appropriate, but…oh, hell, why not?

She took the microphone and cleared her throat. "Okay, y'all need to imagine me in a long, frilly dress, and some seriously big hair, okay?"

"Oh, dear Lord," she thought she heard Justin mutter.

"That would be Loretta Lynn, in case you're not sure," she said.

She took a deep breath and began to sing "You Ain't Woman Enough (To Take My Man)," belting out the words, hoping the gusto instigated by three Tennessee Poodles could balance out her lack of warm-up scales.

The men were grinning, hitting Justin on the arm, but he was just staring at Allie, openmouthed, a half smile working its way into a real smile. She nearly lost her train of thought, seeing him watch her like that, as though he really, seriously did appreciate not only her vocal skills, but the musical selection.

By the time the last line of the song faded into the

night, most of the campers, including Justin, were standing, hooting, and clapping.

Allie was immediately surrounded by the ladies, who said all kinds of nice things like, "We should just run you down to Lower Broadway and drop you off by the Ryman," and "I sure ain't gonna mess with your man. I'm officially scared of you," and "Miss Loretta would give you the keys to the coal mine if she could hear that."

By the time she started back to her seat, Justin had his crutches under his arm and was making his way to the edge of the crowd. The energy of the night made her bold, and she stopped him with two hands full of shirt on either side of his waist. "You runnin' away?" she asked. "Conceding that I am without a doubt the superior vocalist?"

One of the men called from the circle of chairs, "Boy, you better make sure she knows you're not payin' attention to other women!"

And someone else yelled, "You better prove it!"

Justin's eyes were unreadable in the dark.

Allie froze, staring up at him, and the crowd faded into white noise around them.

He dropped one of his crutches as he yanked her forward, completely against his hard chest, and bent his head to hers. Then he kissed not only the daylights, but the night-lights out of her as well.

His mouth was firm and demanding, one hand holding her tight to him as he parted her lips with his own, licking into her mouth. He groaned as she twined her arms around his neck. Her breasts swelled, nipples peaking under the sweatshirt she wore, searching for friction against his body.

Allie vaguely heard someone hoot and call "Get a

camper!" as her world was thoroughly rocked.

Coming up for air, Justin moved his mouth along her jawline and below, his teeth and tongue caressing her neck as he muttered, "Oh, hell, Allie."

She broke away to stare at him. He called her Allie. Not *babe*, not *his girl*. Allie.

She bent to pick up his crutch and hand it to him. Everyone seemed to have lost interest in their interactions, or at least were pretending to give their intimate interlude some privacy, thank God.

Justin didn't meet her eyes as he said, "So, yeah. That was me trying to convince myself that I'm not lusting after you."

"I think that ship set sail in the hot tub last night."

"I'm going to go to hell," he said, leaning his forehead against hers, but not touching her anywhere else.

She laughed and felt happier than she had in years.

Justin didn't look quite so happy. He pulled back and searched her gaze, his eyes dark and bottomless. A reluctant smile crept across his face.

They kissed again, and this time it was sweet and slow.

"You gonna take me inside and take advantage of me?" she asked, finally.

He sighed. "Yeah. I probably am. But I promised these people a song first, and I've got a bet to win."

"You're chicken," she taunted, stepping out of his arms.

"After that"—he aimed his thumb over his shoulder toward the bathhouse—"you're on. Start working on those dippy eggs now."

"Cock-a-doodle-doo." She watched him make his way toward the facilities. Her whole body tingled with a sense of unreality.

Chapter Sixteen

Justin looked at himself in the speckled mirror in the men's restroom as he washed his hands. He splashed water on his face and used half a roll of the world's most nonabsorbent paper towels to dry himself.

"What the fuck are you doing?" he said to the foggy reflection.

"Why, I'm letting my dick do my thinking," he answered himself.

"Well, that's just as well. Your dick has the same number of brain cells as your skull."

A toilet flushed, and a skinny kid about twelve came out of the stall.

"Oh, hell, sorry, bud." Justin said, stepping away from the counter. "Here, you can have the sink."

Eyes wide and hands up, the boy skirted Justin. "That's okay, sir. My mom's got plenty of hand sanitizer back at the tent."

Justin waited a few seconds after the outer door slammed behind the kid before leaving, so the youngster wouldn't have any additional reason to alert his parents that there was a perv on the premises.

He couldn't stay in the can forever, though. He had to face Allie. There was no more pretending that he didn't want to be with her—that boat was long gone from the marina. But no matter how much he wanted her—and how much she thought she wanted him—he couldn't do it.

The imaginary Ghost of Dave arrived and said, "Just because I asked you to look out for her, doesn't mean that you shouldn't treat her like a woman. Jesus, dude, as long as I don't hear the details, do whatever the hell you want, if she's willing."

But that wasn't the point. Allie deserved someone who would stay with her. Someone who didn't need to dive into a forest fire to make sense of things. All Justin could offer her was a roll in the hay. Otherwise, he was adrift, like smoke billowing through the desert. Hell, the only time he felt grounded anymore was when Allie was nearby—

He shook his head, banishing that thought. He pushed the door to the men's room open and went back outside.

By the time he finally got his lame self back to the party, the musical entertainment had changed, and someone was playing guitar. As he got closer, he realized Allie was singing with one of the women.

He stopped outside of the circle of light cast by the fire and listened. His girl really had a fucking beautiful voice. A little husky, a lot sexy.

But not his girl. He wasn't staying; he was just here long enough for his leg to heal, to fix the financial disaster he'd helped get them into, and then run. How was he going to get that through his skull and make it stick?

When the song ended, everyone clapped, and then someone close to the guitarist said something that Justin couldn't hear. He turned to Allie with his eyebrows raised. "You know it?"

Allie grimaced and said, "Not sure I can get through it without crying." Then she shrugged. "It was my brother's favorite, though. I'll give it a shot."

The guitarist started to strum. The opening chords were familiar, but Justin couldn't quite—

It was Garth Brooks's song "The Dance."

Dammit. It wasn't a long song, but it sure packed a punch. As she started to sing the story of a great love ending in heartbreak, he stepped farther back into the shadows.

She must have seen his movement, because she faltered. Her voice cracked, but she looked away from him and pulled it together. Justin wasn't so lucky. God*dammit.

It was a love-gone-wrong song, but it was about so much more—living a life without regrets. It was about memories, just as much as about being in the moment.

He backed up a few more paces, but her voice followed him. The guy on guitar joined in, and their harmony floated over the silent crowd and stabbed Justin in the heart.

Maybe Dave felt the need to send him a message with that song, but he had no idea what the fuck it was—or if he wanted to hear it. He clenched his jaw and stood as close to parade rest as he could manage with one leg and two crutches.

When the voices trailed off into the darkness, there was silence for a moment, then someone started to clap.

Allie watch him the whole time, a silent apology in her eyes.

As the applause died down, someone from the crowd turned and said, "Hey, man, come top that!"

Justin faked a laugh and called back, "We'll be here two more days. I'll get my chance. You old folks need your rest."

He turned toward the camper before he could see anything else in Allie's eyes.

• • •

Damn. Allie knew she shouldn't have sung that song. It was hard enough for her to get through, but as soon as she saw Justin standing there, so lost in his pain, she realized she'd screwed up in a big way.

The camper was dark when she let herself in and shut the door behind her, trying not to make too much noise.

The faint light from the microwave clock illuminated Justin lying on the little couch, one arm thrown over his eyes.

"I'm sorry," she said. "That was hard for you. I just got caught up."

He lowered his arm, eyes glinting in the dark. "It's cool." And put the arm back over the eyes, shutting her out.

"Which is why you're hiding from me."

The arm went back down. "I'm right here. Just tired."

She couldn't let this go. Not after they'd connected out there by the campfire. She would have sat down on the couch, but he was fairly well sprawled over it, his good foot on the floor, knee bent. He left her nowhere to find a place, so she sank down onto the floor and leaned against his leg. He jerked, as though she'd shocked him, and stiffened.

"I think we need to talk about this," she said.

"I don't."

Well, that was clear. She sat for a moment in the dark, feeling the heat of his leg seep through her clothes, warming her in spite of his chilly behavior. She was probably imagining things, but after a moment, she felt him relax a little. It was tempting to just sit there and feel, just touch him, remind him with her body that she wanted him, but she was a talker.

"Here's the thing," she told him. "We're here together, and you want me. You said so. God knows, I want you, too. We're two healthy, unattached adults, and not blood kin, so there's really no reason we can't get busy with each other."

"You're too nice of a girl to have casual sex with, and a few rolls around the camper are all I can offer you. Getting naked with you would be very nice, but—"

Allie cut him off with an elbow to the thigh, then sat back. "You are so full of shit."

He sighed, finally sitting up. "Yes, I am. And you should stay far, far away from me." He scrubbed his hands over his face. "Babe—"

That was enough. "I'm not going to beg. But I am going to tell you this. I care about you. Not just as a friend, and not just as someone I've known my whole life. I want to be with you, and we don't have to involve the rest of the family—we can go our separate ways when we get back to Blue Mountain, no strings attached, or we can fly to Vegas and get married. But I'm not going to sit on my ass and wait forever, and I'm not going to chase you around."

She stood, brushing invisible dirt from her backside. "We're going to be in this camper together for the next week or so. I vote we make the most of the close quarters, no need to trade off with this miserable couch, but it's not up to me. The ball is in your court. Meanwhile, I'll be…masturbating."

She stalked into the bedroom and shut the door as violently as a lightweight sliding door would slam.

The sweatshirt came off with a couple of hearty jerks, and she kicked off one sneaker, then removed the other manually. Unbuttoning her jeans more slowly, she acknowledged to herself that she was too pissed off, frustrated…hurt…to do what she'd just said.

There was silence from the living area. Well, if nothing else, she'd given him something to think about.

Chapter Seventeen

Oh, holy hell.

After a few moments of rustling behind the bedroom door, there was only silence.

The noise in Justin's head took longer to settle. He kept imagining that he heard Allie sigh, or whimper, or shift her legs.

What was she thinking about? Did she have something sexy on that ereader she carried everywhere she went? Maybe she was thinking about him, about what they'd done in the hot tub.

Had she left her panties on? Was her hand sliding under the fabric even now? Maybe she used something, a toy. Nothing battery-operated, though—the dense, motionless air inside the camper couldn't mask the buzz of a vibrator.

He thought about opening the door and watching as she stroked her breast. She would lick one finger before teasing the nipple, circling around like his tongue wanted to do—

while the other hand parted slippery folds, sliding back and forth over her swollen clit.

Did she slip her fingers inside herself, stroking and playing, or just focus on the goal, working to get off quickly? Would she then fall asleep, musk-scented fingers curled under her cheek?

He thrashed around on the couch for a while, his own arousal making it impossible to sleep. He should stroke one off, be done with it, pass out.

Instead, he found himself standing in the bedroom doorway, staring down the length of the bed at Allie where she lay, covered only by a sheet.

What was he doing here? She couldn't possibly want him. Surely she'd have sobered up by now, come to her senses, realized he wasn't right for her—

She swept the sheet away, revealing her legs, long and pale in the filtered moonlight, a shadowed space below the hem of his USMC T-shirt that was clinging to her soft curves. His gaze traveled to the column of her throat, to her lips finally, her wide, solemn eyes. Waiting. Expectant.

He could have stood looking at her forever, but she shifted, reaching for the edge of the T-shirt, pulling it up to reveal…skin.

He maneuvered around to the side of the bed, where she met him, sitting on the edge of the mattress, looking up at him. There was no time to put his crutches aside before she had her hands on his waistband, tugging the elastic of his gym shorts down, freeing his throbbing erection. The cool air on his overheated skin, followed by her warm, smooth fingers, was almost too much.

He grabbed her hand to stop the motion and laughed.

"Jesus, Allie, slow down, or it'll be over before it starts."

She looked up at him, still not smiling. "I'm afraid if I give you two seconds, you'll run away again."

He snorted, in spite of his aching balls. "I don't run away from trouble, Sneezy. I'm a fucking United States Marine."

That got the smile he wanted. Followed by a kiss, right on the head of his cock.

"Oh, fuck me," he groaned when she followed up with a long lick.

"I intend to, in a little bit," she said before sucking him into her mouth.

And she worked him, taking him in, stroking his balls gently in counterpoint to the strong suction of her lips, wrapping her fingers around his length when she couldn't take him all the way—then just focusing on the head, using her lips and tongue to do something that was making sparks gather at the base of his spine—

"Okay, enough," he gasped, pulling her away and collapsing inelegantly next to her on the bed, bringing her lush body to lie next to his.

• • •

Before Allie could catch her breath, Justin was kissing her, drawing her bottom lip between his, ravishing it with licks and nips and sending shock waves to every other nerve ending in her body.

She was on fire. Her nipples ached, finding some relief against the crisp hair of his chest.

While he moved his lips from her mouth to her neck, he pulled her leg over his hip, pressing the length of his erection along her core.

She was almost too wet, she slid over him so easily. But then he rocked against her, and her clit pulsed in response, while she clutched his shoulders and tried to wiggle higher so she could slide him inside.

"Grab a condom out of my seabag," he murmured, raising his head and pointing toward the side of the bed.

Reluctantly rolling away, she fished around off the side of the bed.

He leaned over her shoulder, hot against her back. "Toiletry bag right…there."

She handed the condom to him over her shoulder and started to push herself up, but he stopped her with a hand on her hip.

"Stay right there. Just like that."

She heard the plastic wrapper tear and felt him shifting his leg around behind her as her skin grew tighter, anxious for him to touch her again. She arched against the sheet, whimpering.

"That's it, baby, show me how bad you want it." Rough fingers pushed her hair aside and ran from her neck, over her tattoo, and stopped on her left butt cheek, then offered it a quick, light smack.

"Oh my God, Justin. I want it. I want it so bad." She was nearly sobbing now, her sex clenching, longing to be filled.

"Well then, take it."

She arched her back, offering herself to him, hoping he would—yesssss. He pulled at her hip, moving her partially to her side, with her legs bent forward so he could—

The blunt head of his cock nudged her and she lifted her upper leg enough for him to slide home, right inside her, right *there*.

And then he began to thrust. Shallowly, because their position didn't allow him to go too deep, but God, he was deep enough. And he was going fast. And hard.

The sound of his belly slapping against her buttocks, his muttered curses, the overwhelming reality that she was actually having sex with Justin Morgan, were so overwhelming she didn't think she'd be able to come. Didn't want to, because she'd lose that little bit of consciousness that would take any of this moment away from her memories.

But then he reached around her to touch her clit and said, "I need you to come, Allie. I need to feel you go crazy wild around me. Let me have it. Make this the most perfect night we've both ever had."

And then her body clenched around him for all it was worth, and when she regained her senses, realized she'd lost not only time, but any remaining bits of her heart, as well.

• • •

Justin woke when he heard Allie slide open the door from the bedroom, but didn't open his eyes until she'd done something in the kitchen and then let herself out of the camper. The growl and burble of the coffeemaker followed by the first whiffs of morning brew convinced him to sit up and face the day.

He used the little bathroom in the camper to relieve himself and shave, then debated squeezing into the shower to hose off, but decided he had time to grab a cup of coffee before Allie got back.

His mind was still reeling from what they'd done last

night. Not only had they had sex, they'd had blow-the-roof-off dirty sex. Well. Dirtier than he'd imagined his first time with Allie could be. He'd hoped that a few hours of sleep would add some clarity. If anything, his nightmares had twisted him into further knots. He kept dreaming that he'd gotten up and gone into her room and begun to make love to her, and then turned around to see the whole family standing in the doorway, shaking their heads in disgust. Someone would say, "I thought you were supposed to look out for her." He always woke up in a sweat before he could argue that they were two consenting adults who didn't need anyone's permission to have sex.

He must have repeated the experience three or four times, each time thinking it was real, except that in the dream, his leg wasn't messed up. And Allie told her family, "I just let him in here to get him to quit whining." Like he was a foster dog or something.

Justin had just reached for a mug when the door to the camper opened and Allie stepped in, bringing in the sound of singing birds and chasing out the cobwebs. "G'morning," he said.

"Hey." She glanced at him shyly, then scooted around him and took her things into the bedroom, then came back into the living space for coffee.

Was his girl having morning-after regrets? He'd insisted on fucking her from behind while he panted filth into her ear. Or did she assume he was the one with regrets? *Was he?*

Before he could formulate anything to say that wouldn't be a verbal IED, she pulled a box of Pop-Tarts from the cabinet above the sink. "I'm not sure we have time to cook this morning. You okay with cold carbohydrates?"

"Sure," he said, fine with postponing the "are we okay" discussion. "When do we have to leave?"

"We're supposed to be at Liquor World at ten. That's in forty minutes. Google Maps says it's a fifteen-minute drive."

Justin took a five-second shower while Allie did her hair-dryer magic in the bedroom, even though it tripped a breaker three times. He really couldn't tell the difference between her regular air-dried hair and the blow-dryer version, but it was important to Allie, so finally, he'd stood next to the breaker box and flipped the switch back every time it snapped off until her hair was dry.

They talked business and wardrobe. Justin decided on khaki cargo pants with a zip-off leg for his boot and a knit Blue Mountain shirt. Allie went country, putting on a short—but not silly short—dress with cowboy boots. They made sure the Rainbow Dog flyers were in folders to show the buyers.

When they came out of the camper, one of their new biker friends, who looked like an undernourished Santa Claus, was walking past with a little white dog on a leash.

"Hey, hey, lovebirds!" he called. "Good morning!"

"Good morning, Kyle!" Allie said. How did she remember everyone's name? She didn't look at Justin as she beeped the unlocking mechanism on the car.

They both got in, and she started the engine before turning to look at him. "Look, I hope things aren't going to be weird today."

He met fire with obstinacy, as usual. "Why would things be weird?"

She rolled her eyes. "Because I finally tormented you into having sex with me. I'm glad we did it. It was amazing, but I don't want you to feel obligated or anything."

"If we're going to discuss this now, you need to pour a couple of shots of Brown Dog in my travel mug," he told her. "But I don't think that will go over well with your potential investors."

"Don't be a dick," she said, frustration clouding her eyes.

Shit. "You're overthinking things." He didn't want her to be mad at him, but better mad than hurt, at least until he figured out his own head.

Allie snorted and put the car into gear. "I'm totally going back in time and falling for Brandon."

Justin laughed, in spite of himself. Damn her, for being so fucking cute.

· · ·

"Well, that was uninspiring," Allie said after their second meeting of the morning. She was disappointed, but determined to be optimistic. They'd stopped for lunch at a Bar-B-Cutie outside Nashville. She bit into her barbecued pork sandwich and chewed.

Justin poked at his brisket and shrugged. "It was a definite conditional maybe," he said.

"Not exactly something we can take to the bank."

"Hey, they said they'd give you shelf space if you make it."

"But they weren't interested in making even a partial investment if it didn't come with Blue Mountain Bourbon's seal of approval."

Again, the unconcerned shrug, which was starting to annoy her.

She huffed out a breath. Surely he knew what the stakes were here? If they didn't get an investor, he was going to wind up throwing himself on the sword of his father's mercy… or something like that…to help cover that deductible. She'd half hoped that he might change his mind—realize that he did love Blue Mountain and want to stay—but it was clearer by the day that there was more to Justin's rush to leave than his alienation from his dad. He was home from the Middle East, but he still had a war to fight, and didn't think he could fight it at home.

So why didn't he seem so worried that they hadn't found an investor for Rainbow Dog yet?

He scratched his chin. "I dunno, we can use that maybe from the last meeting as leverage for the next guy. Surely we can spin it into some sort of a 'We've got several other distributors interested, if we can find terms that everyone's comfortable with.'"

She grumbled, "Terms like 'Give us anything, anything at all that will cover our costs just so we can get our product on the bottom shelf'?"

Justin laughed, the little lines at the corners of his eyes appearing for the first time that day. "If I didn't know you better, I might think that was sarcasm."

Allie slurped her diet soda. She put her chin on her fist. "I have to believe we can get this to work. People just have to decide that it's hip."

She thought about how to explain herself. At least they were talking comfortably again. She was kicking herself for what she'd said last night. *Any way I can get you.* Sheesh. Run away! Keep running! I'll probably chase you, anyway!

"I gotta hand it to you," Justin said, obviously unaware

of her thoughts. "You charmed the socks off that lady at Liquor World."

"Yeah, after she conned me out of three pints of free Rainbow Dog preserves to use in her Cooking With Booze demo."

"Hey, if they order that from us, for all their stores? That's a sale, and it's not like it was expensive to make."

Allie shrugged. He was right. The preserves weren't preserves at all, not in the traditional sense. All she'd done was to take a jar of Sherry's homemade jam, mix in some white dog, and put it in a different jar. Add a pretty lid on it and a clever label about how Rainbow Dog preserves went with anything...ice cream, corn bread, biscuits... All she had to do was figure out how to put it into pie, and she'd have drunken desserts from Cincinnati to Mobile.

It wasn't exactly what she envisioned for her product, but as a side effort, it would be okay.

"Well, keep your chin up, babe. You'll come up with something. I have faith in you."

Huh. Even though he was either boiling or frigid in the nooky department, he did still seem to believe she could pull this off. That was huge.

"Where do we go next?"

Allie chewed her lip for a moment. Their next two appointments had canceled on them. One bar mogul, who owned four bars and restaurants in Nashville, had said he just didn't see a market for raw bourbon, that he already carried a couple brands of moonshine. The other one had just left a message saying not to come.

Finally, she fessed up. "We don't have anything else today."

"Oh. Well, should we go back and pack up the camper and go to Memphis?"

"We can't check in at the next campground until tomorrow. It was booked." They were stuck with each other for the next eighteen hours or so, with nowhere to go.

"Want to go to a movie or something?"

Well, that was nice. At least he wasn't suggesting that he catch a Greyhound bus back to Crockett County. "We should go back to the campground. I need to make some more calls, and I left the binder with the contact list in the camper."

"Okay," Justin said.

She thought he would have been more reluctant to go "home" with her with nothing planned for the day, but he was probably tired. That was fine; so was she. They could take turns napping on the big bed.

Allie couldn't hope there'd be more going on in that bed than sleep, because everything about his demeanor screamed that last night was a one-off. He'd hang around until they got Rainbow Dog off the ground—or buried, because he'd promised. But then he'd go.

If for no other reason, she had to find some way to land an investor, so he could get out West, away from all the reminders of Dave, and move on with his life.

Chapter Eighteen

Justin was tempted to tell Allie what he'd done, just to get a spring back into her step. He'd made a few calls and put things in motion that would have her silent partner signed, sealed, and delivered in just a few days…but he really wanted her to have a chance to pitch the business plan in person to Merilee, so that Allie'd know it was her project—her work, her pitch, her business acumen—that sealed the deal.

They drove into the campground without speaking, slowly rolling past the other campsites. People were out and about, walking dogs, sitting and talking. A couple of guys tinkered with their bikes, tools spread out on a picnic table.

One of the guys hailed them. "Hey, have you all been in town?" he asked. "I promised Pinky I'd take him, and I can't get this damned GPS to work. I know you just got back, but Justin, if you feel up to it, would you mind coming along and navigating? I promise we'll only be gone an hour or two." He winked at Allie. "I'll have him back before you miss him too much."

Perfect. He had a phone call to make somewhere Allie wouldn't overhear.

· · ·

"Hey, babe," Justin said to Merilee's voicemail forty minutes later. "It's Justin Morgan. Just checking to make sure you're going to be at On the Rocks next week. Be careful about calling back or sending texts. I don't want Allie to know what we've got going on. I'll try to catch you again later."

He hung up and followed the guys into in the waiting area of a real, live, old-fashioned barbershop, where he spent the next hour listening to old men gossip.

He was having a surprisingly good time. At first he was annoyed that he'd been tricked into coming to a fucking barbershop, that the boys knew their way into town. He reminded them that he hadn't lost his bet. Yet. But they assured him they just wanted his company. They'd been coming to this particular barbershop every year for the past twenty. It was a ritual stop on their annual pilgrimage. Apparently one of the guys didn't get a single hair cut between visits.

"Although," chimed in the barber, "every year when he comes in here, the job is easier, because there's just not quite as much to cut each time."

The conversation turned to a few people who weren't there. There was silence then, for a moment, the implication that they'd be seeing a new grave marker when they stopped at Arlington at the end of their journey.

It freaked Justin out how casually they discussed death. Like it was a relative they didn't much like, but that they tolerated.

"Your girl says you're stopping in DC on the way home from your booze festival gig," one of the guys said.

Justin stiffened. "I don't think so." He shoved his overgrown bangs out of his eyes. The hair that Allie griped about.

"She seemed pretty set on it."

He didn't answer. Why she was so determined to push him into going to Dave's grave was beyond him. He didn't need to see the marker to know Dave was gone. But maybe it wasn't for him at all. It was for her.

How had he managed to forget Dave wasn't just his best friend? He'd been Allie's big brother. And hell. Justin had lost him two years ago... Allie had lost him long before that, when he'd enlisted and left home.

She didn't have as much crap hanging over her head, either. Didn't have to know what those last minutes had been like for Dave, the part that Justin had played in the end...but shit. She would probably handle that better, too, and never need a VA shrink to tell her she had to deal with survivor's grief.

Jesus. He was such a self-centered asshole.

The old marine slapped him on the arm and said, "You ready to hit the road home?"

"Just a minute," Justin answered, then turned to the barber. "You got time for one more before you turn the closed sign around?"

Chapter Nineteen

Justin was embarrassingly nervous when he got out of the car. His nerves weren't helped by the fact that he felt flushed to the roots of his hair, and those roots were pretty exposed right now.

Jesus. When he'd told the barber that he wouldn't mind a regulation haircut, he didn't mean the basic training version.

Afterward, he'd mentioned that Allie had had a bad morning, and that he'd been an asshole in general, and she was probably pissed off at him. So he'd been browbeaten into buying a conciliatory picnic supper, complete with wine and flowers.

Based on the look in her eye as she approached him, his last chance to stay out of Allie McGrath's panties was about to be gone with the wind.

"Hey," she said when she got to him. She wore jeans and a long-sleeved Blue Mountain T-shirt that complemented the green in her eyes.

"How was your afternoon?" he asked.

She nodded. "Okay."

He wanted to push her hair behind her ear, but one hand was full of apology supplies, and the other was doing everything it could to hold him upright.

"Thanks for navigating," the driver said, moving toward his wife, who was sitting at a nearby card table with a number of the other women.

"You're welcome," Justin said, not looking at him. He couldn't stop staring at Allie. He didn't know what had changed since he'd been gone. He thought maybe it was him.

"So...do you need help with your stuff there?" she asked.

"Oh! Yes. I, um, shit." He handed her the bag. "I, uh, got you flowers. But you can kind of see that, I guess."

"Well, I do see the flowers," she said, reaching into the bag and pulling them out. She buried her nose in them, though she wouldn't smell anything. They were some kind of chintzy daisy thing, and an artificial fluorescent color at that, but they were the only ones the grocery store had. "I didn't want to presume."

He said, "Well, I prefer roses, if I'm going to get flowers for myself, but I thought you probably preferred weird, mutant, semi-artificial flowers."

She smiled, the heat in her eyes unmistakable. "I do now."

He cleared his throat. "So, I got some food for supper, too. But I kind of need to take a shower before we eat, if that's okay."

Allie sighed. "I suppose it would be unpleasant for me to have to pick newly shorn hair shreds out of my food while you sit there and scratch all through supper."

He drew a deep breath.

It was going to be okay. Whatever happened between them in the next few hours would probably be okay, because she *was* his girl. His Allie. They might be lovers, and if she hadn't changed her mind, still wanted to be with him, even though she knew he was leaving to go out West and was okay with that, then he was all in. Or she might have come to her senses and realized what a head case he was and decided to back off. That would be okay, too. He hoped like hell she chose the first option.

She was the coolest, toughest girl he knew, and she'd be okay.

It occurred to him, as he waited for her to take the shopping bag inside and get his shower things for the camp facilities, that maybe Dave had asked him to look out for her not because *she* needed *Justin's* help, but because Dave knew that *Justin* needed *her*. And not just in some freaky premonition-of-bum-leg kind of way.

. . .

He got his freaking hair cut. And bought flowers. Did that mean something? Allie felt like it meant something. Like he was apologizing for pulling away from her after last night. Either that, or he was conceding that she was the supreme goddess of karaoke and was too embarrassed to sing in public after his boasting last night.

But what if it meant more? Like, something romantic. She was obsessing, anyway, in spite of trying to keep herself busy unloading flowers. And the fancy cheese with even fancier crackers, and—oh, hell—wine and chocolates. There were some kind of sandwiches, wrapped in pretty paper, and gourmet kettle-cooked potato chips.

Allie dropped the pastry box back in the bag and ran to the little bathroom, where she combed her hair and took the world's quickest sponge bath to be sure everything about her was fresh and clean. Not that she was expecting it to get there. More like insurance that it wouldn't. Because, really. The likelihood of Justin finally deciding he wanted to get naked with her again was probably inversely correlated with the state of her hygiene. As in, he would only tell her he wanted her to take off her clothes if she was so dirty and stinky that he could be sure that she would refuse.

She shoved her jeans and T-shirt in the closet and put on a soft, clingy-knit sundress, then took it back off again, feeling like that was too desperate. Then put it back on. Looking nice would probably provide the same anti-Justin armor as bathing.

The door to the camper opened, and Justin began to make his slow journey up the steps.

She took a breath, stepping out where she could see him. With that short hair, his already square jaw was like steel, and his blue eyes glowed with a laser-like intensity. "God, you look handsome," she blurted.

He just stared at her for a moment. His eyes traveled from her hair, which she automatically tucked behind her left ear, over her face, pausing at her lips, down the center of her body, lingering at her chest. Her nipples felt his gaze and swelled in response. She started to cross her arms over them, then stopped, and his mouth quirked, before his gaze dropped to caress her stomach, hips, thighs, finally resting on her feet, causing him to grin widely.

"What?" She looked down. "Oh." She'd left on her "My sock" and "My other sock" socks. Which had a big hole in one toe.

"You look really pretty," he said, and there was more in his eyes, something he probably wasn't quite ready to say out loud. Which was fine, because she wasn't sure she was ready to hear it.

Allie nearly wept. As it was, her heart hiccuped before beating a little harder and faster than usual. "I feel like this is kind of a date, or something," she said, then wanted to kick herself.

To cover her awkwardness, she took his toiletry bag, the one with the condoms in it, and tossed it into the bedroom, on top of his seabag.

But he nodded when she turned back to him. "Yeah. I uh, I kind of do, too. Feel like we're dating." He approached her, slowly, warily.

"I won't bite you," she said.

"That's a shame."

It took a good two-tenths of a second before she was up against him, her arms around his neck, lips pressed to his. Her mouth opened under his, tongue slipping out to taste his; the textures and heat made her knees go weak. He wrapped one arm around her waist, pulling her against him, nibbling at her mouth, his lips and teeth and tongue devouring. She tried to reciprocate while running one hand through his stubbled hair, afraid if she let him go he'd disappear.

Turning with him, she pushed him down onto the couch, stepped out of the way of his bum leg, then looked down into his serious blue eyes, so full of...want.

She took his remaining crutch and leaned it against

the wall. After a deep breath, she pulled her dress to the tops of her thighs. His eyes went to the juncture of her legs, and his lips parted, tongue sliding out to lick his bottom lip. Inelegantly, she climbed over him, a knee on either side of his legs. His hands immediately spanned her waist, pulling her down against his crotch, his hard length pressing against her core, right—oh God—right there.

Her whimper echoed his sigh when she writhed against him. Swollen and wet with need, almost exactly where she needed to be, she stared down into his widened blue eyes.

She didn't kiss him again, not just yet. She reached for the hands that curved around her hips and moved them up, over her rib cage, to her heavy and achy breasts, which were in need of a man's touch. This man. He finally pulled the straps of her dress down and cupped her, licked one nipple, then the other. Then took the first into his mouth, pulling strongly.

An exceptionally strong tug on her nipple had her grabbing his shoulders and arching against him, crying out for more.

He was aligned so closely that even through layers of fabric, she had to move only a few millimeters to feel the head of his cock press against her clit, enough to send waves of electric heat from her head to her feet.

"Oh, Jesus, hold still," he said.

"But I need…you in me, now," she said, hearing the desperation in her own voice.

"Fuck," he said, and moved his hands off her breasts and pushed her away from where their bodies met. "No—"

Her laughter held a note of hysteria. She couldn't help it. She scooted off him, flopped down on the couch next to him.

"Of course not. I knew that." Hell, she'd taken out shower insurance.

"Not completely." He ran a hand over his shorn hair. "Condoms. In the other room."

"Here." She grabbed her purse from the table, pulling out her Hope Chest, the little plastic box that she kept spare tampons—and, yes, condoms—in.

That Justin Morgan smile appeared as he opened it.

She took one of the little packets out and waved it by one corner.

The little case landed on the floor as he grabbed the condom and turned to lay her back against the couch, kissing her, tongue sweeping into her mouth, tangling with hers.

"Holy shit, babe, I'm going to fuck you blind."

She hesitated half of a second at his use of "babe." As long as she remembered that she wasn't special, this would be just fine. Better than fine. "It's about damned time," she said, pulling his shirt out of his waistband.

Chapter Twenty

Justin's hands shook when he pushed Allie's dress above her thighs and revealed the cotton panties she wore. No thong today. He thought these were called boy shorts or something; they were straight across her legs and belly, but made her look like anything but a boy. Thank God. She arched, undulating restlessly.

She watched him, eyes hooded, tongue peeking out to wet her lips. He must have been staring, because she said, "Here's where you either pull off your drawers or I do it. At least I think that's what's supposed to happen. I've seen a couple of movies where they did something similar."

God, he loved her smart mouth.

"I tell you what," she continued. "Since you seem to be paralyzed with indecision, I'll take care of exposing myself. You think you can handle getting your business ready?"

Squirming, she tucked her thumbs into the waistband of the panties, thrusting her pelvis into the air in order to work them over her backside.

He rocketed into action, unbuttoning his fly with a minimum of fumbling. His dick was so hard he had difficulty with the zipper, but he managed, somehow, to get his pants and boxers halfway down his thighs, almost to his ankle brace.

"That's good enough," Allie said.

And damn. He'd missed the unveiling. She was curled up, hugging her knees while she watched him try to undress. "Lose the dress," he demanded. It was half off her shoulders already, nearly bunched around her waist.

And then there she was. Leaning back, completely naked except for the socks, right next to him.

His cock leaped with joy and agony. He still had the condom, so he tore it open and covered himself.

This couch was too damned short, barely big enough to hold him; it was definitely too small for two adults to have sex, but he wasn't going to suggest they move to the bedroom.

He scooted as far to the end as he could so she could lie back. She draped one leg on the back of the couch, making room for his hips between hers, and damn if that didn't leave her wet and open to his viewing pleasure.

But he didn't stare at her pussy as he touched her—he watched her face, as she watched him slide two fingers along her opening, spreading the slick evidence of her desire. She sighed when he pushed his fingers inside her, and he twitched in response.

"Do you think we could save the 'getting reacquainted with our sexy parts' for later? I really, really need to feel you in me," she gasped.

He moved his fingers in and out again, brushing her clit with his thumb, resting it there, feeling it pulse. "I don't know," he said. "What if you decide you don't want me after this? I might never get another chance."

She laughed, and she contracted around his fingers. "I promise. I swear to God, I'll let you in at least one more time."

This wasn't like last night, hot and desperate in the dark—which had been earth-shattering for him, but he wasn't sure about her, and he wanted to make sure this time was special for Allie.

"Jus-tin!" she moaned.

He was dying to be there, but Jesus, what if he came right away, and she didn't get off? God, he felt like a damned virgin, but it had never been like this in the backseat of his dad's Chrysler. No, this was Allie, and he could tell her the truth.

He slid his fingers in again, curling up, searching for her sweet spot. Moving his thumb again. "I've got a touch of performance anxiety," he said. "If I go off too early, I want to make sure you're taken care of."

"You weren't so worried about this last night. You were all, 'Come now, Allie, I said so,' and I sure managed to get off."

He stopped the motion of his fingers, smoothed them over her pubis, finally looked her in the eye. "This is different."

"Oh." Damn those deep green eyes.

"I want to learn you, baby. I want to know everything that makes you squirm, pant, sigh, what makes you wet. For as long as I'm here, as long as you'll let me, I'm gonna be the best lover you ever had. I'm going to do everything you want."

That was the God's honest truth. The other truth that he didn't bother to mention—no need to totally kill the mood—was that he wasn't sure how he was going to manage being on top with this ankle brace taking up so much room.

"Well, in that case, sit back, because I want to fuck your brains out."

And all of his concerns about where he was going to put his damned leg brace shot out of his mind, because she pushed him back on the seat and straddled him again, grasping his cock and sliding—oh, fuck—sliding right down, all the way— "Oh, fuck."

"Exactly." She put her forearms on his shoulders, holding on to the back of the couch for leverage. She raised and lowered herself, her wet heat surrounding him, driving him to the top immediately.

He grabbed her hips, probably too tightly, because she gasped. But he had to hold her still, because no matter what she said, he was going to make sure she came.

"Stay there. Just like that," he commanded, holding her a few inches above him. He began to thrust upward, slowly, building a rhythm, his thumb going back to her clit, like that was where it belonged. She quivered, muscles tensing around him.

"Yessss," she hissed, head going back, torso arched toward him. He didn't have a free hand to touch those breasts, but he had a mouth, so he managed to catch a nipple and suck, hard, causing her to cry out.

"I need more," she said. Taking his hands in hers, she put them over her breasts. He caught her nipples between his fingers as he caressed her. She stared straight into his eyes as she licked her finger and lowered it to where their bodies were joined.

She was barely moving now, just a slow wave of heat pulsing around his aching cock, but he could feel her fingers moving over her clit as she said, "This is not about your world-famous stud capabilities, or who gets off when. This is about you and me, showing each other how we feel. And I'm showing you that I feel—oh God." Her pussy contracted around him, and heat condensed in his lower spine, spreading up, forward. "Showing you—" She completely lost it then, groaning, clenching him inside her.

And then, if she said anything else, it was lost, because he was coming, blasting off, the top of his head landing somewhere north of Cleveland, the entire rest of his existence wrapped around, and in, this woman.

• • •

The aftershocks lasted way longer than Allie would have imagined, considering her thighs were totally cramped. Somehow she continued to move on Justin's still-hard penis, even though he was trying to push her off him.

"Leaking," he said.

"Oh, shit." She wriggled backward, trying to get her wobbly legs to lift her away as he reached between them to catch the condom.

Sure enough, when he pulled it off and held it up, there was a big, gaping tear about halfway down.

"Ahhh!" Allie reached for a roll of paper towels, tearing one off and throwing it at him. "Wrap it up, wrap it up!"

Justin started to laugh, lying there sprawled out, mostly

naked, holding a dripping condom in one hand, the other hand beneath it to catch what dripped. "It's not a spider," he said.

"No, it's not, it's a—a—potential grandchild maker for Lorena. Oh, hell no!" She leaned down to pick up the paper towels she'd thrown, which hadn't made it to Justin. She leaned her body away and held the towel out to him. He took it and dealt with the offending article, then tossed it into the plastic grocery bag she found for him.

Justin lifted his hips, balancing on his good foot, and pulled his pants back up, but didn't zip or button them. She was totally distracted from her freak-out. God, he was beautiful, all muscles and skin and tattoos, and muscles…

"Hey. You gonna stand there staring at me, or are we gonna bask in post-sex glow for a while?" He looked her up and down. "Although if you just want to stand there for a while and let me look, I can probably be up for round two before you know it."

Allie realized she was standing in the middle of his family's camper, stark naked, holding a trash bag full of broken condom. The effects of which she suddenly felt, tickling the inside of her right thigh.

"Ack!" she shrieked, bolting for the bathroom. She cleaned up, then scrambled into the bedroom to find some clothes. She wasn't thinking about anything, couldn't think of anything besides finding her favorite Kentucky Unbridled T-shirt. She wouldn't think past this moment. There was sperm inside her. Probably heading upstream already, finding an errant egg, which would become…a disaster, because Justin would feel compelled to marry her, and then he would resent her, and then they would both be miserable, and the kid would need therapy, and—she was pulling up fresh panties when the door slid open.

"Don't get dressed on my account," Justin said, waggling his eyebrows at her. He moved into the tiny space, sucking half of the oxygen out of the room.

"I have to get dressed. We have to…do something."

"Like find condoms that were made in this century?" From his pocket, he retrieved the wrapper from the faulty prophylactic. "How long have you had these?"

She thought. "Um…" Since right after college, because that was when she'd gone off the pill because it made her sick, and… "I guess probably for a long time."

He leaned his crutches against the wall as he sat on the mattress, leaning back onto the pillows. He patted the space next to him. "Can you come here for a minute?"

"Maybe?" She was completely off-kilter, and clinging to Justin right now sounded a little too appealing.

"It's okay, babe. We'll talk about it. Later. But I'm not done with you yet." His calm in the midst of her storm was a fulcrum to spin out of control around. But then he leaned back on the bed and reached for his toiletry bag.

Damn, she wasn't done with him yet, either. Oh, what the hell. She could cling for a bit, deal with reality later. She couldn't help but notice that he still hadn't zipped or buttoned his pants, so when he turned, his shorts slid down, revealing the boxer briefs—hugging his perfect backside. And she also couldn't help but slide her hand down inside, over the soft knit fabric—

"Hey, are you copping a feel?" He rolled to his back and pulled her with him, trapping her hand, cupping one delicious buttock.

She squeezed.

He returned the favor.

· · ·

Several hours later, Allie woke from a dream in which she had a baby in a sling carrier, and was trying to earn a living selling lemonade from a stand in front of her house — and her mother kept driving by, looking the other way, never stopping to buy lemonade. And the baby cried, because its daddy drove by and never stopped, either.

"Justin, wake up. We have to talk about this."

"Huh? Wha?" He shot straight up, looking around wildly. "What's wrong?"

"We have to talk."

He blinked at her. "I was sleeping. Like, really sleeping."

"I'm sorry."

He grinned, teeth gleaming through the darkness. "That's okay. Really. I bet I can do it again."

She wondered for a moment if she should worry about that statement, but she was having her own nervous breakdown at the moment.

"What if I'm pregnant?"

"Babe. It'll be okay." He lay back down.

A shiver ran down her spine. "Don't you understand the implications?" Why wasn't he freaking out with her?

Justin stilled, then sat back up, flipping on the light. He stared at her for one moment, then another. There was something going on behind those blue eyes, something Allie didn't recognize, and his jaw was working, biting the inside of his cheek. He looked a little shell-shocked, but not nearly as panicked as she felt.

"What?" she asked. "What's wrong?"

"Would it be so horrible?"

"Being pregnant?"

"Yeah. Having a baby."

Allie flopped over. "What the hell am I going to do with a baby?"

"Buy it cute little UK T-shirts? When it gets a little older, I hear you can teach it to fetch things from the fridge."

Her world was in huge, undulating upheaval, and he was making jokes about kids? "Seriously? What is *wrong* with you?"

"Okay. We can get U of L shirts, too. Wildcats, Cardinals, I don't care, as long as it's healthy. Not Tennessee, though, okay?"

She just glared.

He sighed and pulled her against him, enfolding her in his arms. She lay next to him, but couldn't relax. He kept talking. "We could do that. Be parents."

Pushing away, she stared at him. "Together. You and me. Having a baby."

He nodded, shrugging. "Why not?"

She sat up all the way then. "This is crazy."

He ignored that. "You do know that this naked stuff"— he waved back and forth between them—"is occasionally followed by parenthood, right? You took health at Crockett County High, right?"

"God, yes. Duh. But…that's what the condom was for."

"Okay," Justin said. He reached for his crutches. "My bad. I guess I thought—" He shook his head.

"Thought what?" Now Allie's mind was traveling down

paths she hadn't dared notice before.

"Never mind." He shook his head, but didn't look at her directly.

"No, what did you think?"

"Jesus. Okay. That whole, 'we can go to Vegas' thing was a hyperbole, I get that. But on the other hand, I wouldn't have brought you fucking flowers if I wasn't willing to explore that possibility."

Her heart thunked while she tried to get her lungs to function. Wasn't this the same man who'd pointed out last night, in no uncertain terms, that she had no business counting on him to stick around? She wondered if there had been any brain surgery or hallucinogenic styling products involved with that haircut.

All of the breath in Allie's lungs left as his eyes held her captive. "We had sex twice, and you want to get married? Isn't that supposed to be my line?"

He pinched the bridge of his nose. "No. Not necessarily, I mean—I don't fucking know. But Jesus, Allie, you're— you're fucking Allie! I wouldn't have gone all the way with you if I wasn't willing to—go all the way with you!"

Chapter Twenty-One

Justin pocketed the business card that Marty handed him, then shook his hand and wished him a good trip. He wasn't about to take him up on his offer of meeting up again in a week to visit Arlington, but he'd save the phone number and email address.

Allie shared hugs and tears with the women, whom she'd known all of forty-eight hours. How did women do that instant friendship thing? Whatever. He was glad she'd connected.

He was anxious to get on the road. Their next stop was outside Memphis, and he had a hankering for some ribs. All that sex over the past twenty-four? thirty-six? hours had completely drained him of protein reserves. He'd awakened craving eggs, and all they had were a few slices of leftover cheese and that box of Pop-Tarts from the other morning.

Who went on a camping trip without packing real food?

Next time, Justin was going to be in charge of provisions.

Allie could be in charge of…well, it wouldn't be condoms. Or food. Toothpaste and deodorant, maybe. And paper products. She could do that.

He had to remind himself he was leaving. Assuming that he wasn't going to be a father in the next nine months or so. But what were the odds? Pretty slim, right?

He'd probably overshot the mark last night, talking about the future. But for some reason, when Allie'd panicked over the possibility of an unplanned pregnancy, he'd pictured a round-cheeked little girl with curly red hair and green eyes, whose first words might very well be "Dammit, Daddy!"

And the mental artillery fire that usually kicked up whenever he thought about white board fences around rolling bluegrass fields was silent.

Marty nudged Justin as Allie finally detached from the women with promises to connect on Facebook and to post recipes for something or other on Pinterest (whatever the hell that was). "Earth to Stud Muffin," he said. "You take care of that girl, you hear?"

Justin started, hearing that request, so similar to Dave's last words to him. "Yeah. I'm gonna try."

"And take care of you, too. It's okay if you do. You know, take care of yourself and live a long, healthy life." Some of the desert sand and gunfire settled back into his thoughts, bringing things back into the gritty focus he was accustomed to.

"Yeah. All right." He had to get away. Marty was going to want to have a group hug and sing "Kumbaya" here pretty soon.

"You ready?" Allie approached gingerly. She was moving a little slowly this morning.

"Everything's hooked up and ready to go," he said, indicating Marty. "We just double-checked it all."

"You driving?" she asked, blushing.

"You okay, darlin'?" Marty asked.

"Um, yeah. I just, um, slipped and pulled a muscle," she said. "I'm sure a couple of extra ibuprofen and a nap will fix me up."

Marty shot Justin a look, with a raised eyebrow.

He didn't let his expression change, but suspected his own skin was a little pinker than usual. He wasn't about to admit that there had been an accident involving a crutch and a bottle of chocolate syrup and nakedness. He was incredibly grateful he wouldn't have to explain that one to an emergency room doctor, too.

They got into the camper and waved good-bye to their new friends.

Allie made him stop the motor home by the entrance so she could take a picture of the sign for the campground. "For posterity," she said.

"So Allie Junior will be able to see where she was conceived?" he asked.

"Omigod. Just shut up and drive."

• • •

Allie slept for about two and a half hours of the three-hour drive from Nashville to Memphis. She'd eaten nearly as much breakfast as Justin had, going back for seconds at the breakfast buffet where they'd stopped before getting on the interstate.

She'd apologized before she abandoned the front seat

for the bed in the back, but Justin promised that he didn't mind. "You get some rest. You might need some extra energy later," he said, waggling his eyebrows at her.

As she slowly awoke to the sounds of Justin singing something that sounded vaguely like Blake Shelton, she thought that maybe she had everything she'd ever wanted, right this very minute.

Well, she still wanted to prove to her family that she was an adult, someone to be taken seriously, by making her project successful, all by herself. Herself and one smoking-hot sidekick.

And someday she wanted more. She wanted the husband, the kids—she flashed on the thought of a couple of little Justins bouncing around. She put her hand over her lower belly, wondering what it would feel like to be pregnant. She didn't think she was right now, but... Her last period had ended a few days ago, and that condom had barely leaked. Best not to get too caught up in the fantasy.

"Hey! Sleeping Beauty," Justin called from the front of the camper. "Where's that paper with the reservation info on it?"

"I'm coming," she said.

"Wait until we're at the campground. I want to come, too."

"What have I done? If we'd just kept our genitals separate, how many dumb puns could we have avoided?" she asked as she made her way to the front of the camper and sat in the passenger seat.

His eyes left the road long enough to wiggle his eyebrows again. "Or maybe, we don't have to wait. If you scooted down there between the seats, you could probably—"

"Better be careful, Sport. I might just call your bluff," Allie said.

But then they had reached their exit, and her map-reading skills were more important than her oral abilities, at least for a while.

Their phones chimed almost simultaneously with incoming calls. Since Justin was driving, Allie saw her screen first.

She gave herself one extra ring to have a microscopic panic attack before answering. "Hi, Mom! How's the cruise?"

"Allegra, what's going on there?"

"Oh, wow, that sounds great. So lots of fun in the sun, huh?"

"Allegra..."

She sighed. Justin glanced at her while he hit his own "ignore button" and returned his eyes to the road.

Lorena continued. "We're in port, and when Clyde checked his phone, it had imploded with messages. From the insurance agent and fire inspector and contractor."

Through a frozen brain, Allie heard herself say, "Really? Why would they call Justin's dad? Justin and I have been in contact with everyone, and we've got things completely under control."

Justin's shoulders stiffened, and his jaw muscle ticked.

"From the middle of nowhere?"

"Huh? No, we know exactly where we are. Where did you say you are right now?"

"Stop playing games. We trusted you to be mature enough to keep the distillery intact while we were gone for a very short time, and you've not only destroyed a perfectly good building, but run away from your responsibilities."

Allie winced. "Like I said, Mom, we've got it all taken care of. I'm sure the contractor told Clyde that the rickhouse will be back in business again before we know it, and that we have the deductible taken care of—"

"And that deductible came from D—"

"Mom, you're breaking up. I think we're losing our connection. Mom?" Allie hung up before her mother could say anything else damning, and when the phone rang again, she sent the call to voicemail.

Proving her mother's contention, that yes, Allie was immature and incapable of dealing with life like an adult.

"Shit fuck damn," she said, knocking her head into the window and closing her eyes. They needed to find an investor more than ever now. If she wasn't pregnant, she needed to make sure Justin didn't feel obligated to stick around and work for his father in order to pay her back so that she could get Rainbow Dog launched. She'd rather put the business on the back burner than see him be miserable in a job he hated every day.

If she was pregnant, though…if she was pregnant, she'd need money to take care of herself and a baby…maybe with Justin, if he were serious about sticking around, in a job he liked…maybe he could be a firefighter, or even a cop at home, if he was so determined to stay in some sort of warrior protector-guy job.

The motor home rolled to a stop, and Allie looked up to see that Justin had pulled off the road and into the parking lot of a strip mall.

He picked up his own phone and said, "I guess I'd better call my dad now, huh?"

• • •

But all his dad said was, "Brandon assured me that you've got it all under control. We can discuss the finer points of financing when we're all back at Blue Mountain. Your mother was just calling to make sure you're okay, but she's off getting a spa treatment right now."

"Okay…" This made Justin nervous. His dad was never easygoing about distillery business. There was something else going on. Did Clyde think he could trap Justin with sweetness and convince him to stay home to work for the families? "Hey, Dad, is Brandon around? He left me a couple of messages I didn't get a chance to return."

There was silence at the other end of the line.

"Dad?"

Clyde cleared his throat. "Brandon took a day trip on the island today."

"Oh. So where is he? Whale watching? Visiting a museum?"

"I think he said zip-lining."

It was Justin's turn to be quiet while he contemplated that news.

"That's what I thought, too," Clyde said, and Justin laughed—a rare moment of agreement that his safety-conscious, bookish brother zinging through the tropics on a clothesline was one of the craziest things he'd heard in a while.

• • •

"Damn," Allie said, slapping her leather portfolio against her thigh. "Memphis was a bust, and the first half of our appointments in Atlanta were a waste of time. I thought those guys would want to buy into Rainbow Dog for sure. Especially after how much they sampled it!"

"Hang in there," Justin said. He had to distract her, keep her spirits up. He couldn't tell her that Merilee was a 99.9 percent sure thing, because he wanted to see her do it on her own, but she was starting to look desperate.

Well, sex always kept his mind off his troubles. He put his arm around her as they walked back to the car. He'd reached the two-week mark in his recovery and was down to one crutch. He felt like a new man. The bruise on his chest from the rickhouse fire was just a green-and-yellow memory at this point. The freedom to use his arms was electrifying. Especially since he could use the hand attached to one of those arms, any time he wanted, to touch Allie.

He'd turned into a total sap. Allowing himself to touch her was bringing out a level of corny he wasn't completely uncomfortable with, which bothered the living shit out of him.

He needed to go to the gym. A boxing gym. A stinky, man-sweat-filled, jockstrap-displaying boxing gym. Where he could beat the hell out of a heavy bag and spit and scratch.

After he got Allie back to the camper and cheered her up with strawberries dipped in chocolate and kisses over every inch of her body.

"Can we stop by a store?" he asked.

"A grocery store? A toy store? A hardware store?"

"Hmmm. Any of those could prove interesting, but I was thinking more like a condom and stuff store."

"Shhh!" She waved at him to keep his voice down. "Sure. Maybe we could find one attached to a grocery store so I can pick up some things for supper while you're getting...other stuff?"

For a woman who was so wild behind closed doors, she could be charmingly circumspect about discussing some of the finer points of their intimacy. "Don't you want to go with me to help me pick out what to get? Colors? Flavors? Ribbed or not?"

"No, actually. I'll trust your judgment. After all, my last choice wasn't very reliable."

"Your last choice expired in 2010." He pulled her in for a kiss. "Come with me. It'll be fun. Besides. You helped use up the last of the unexpired stock."

"I am not going condom shopping with you. Everyone will know we're going to have sex!"

A middle-aged woman pushing a toddler-containing stroller hurried past them, shooting Allie an annoyed look.

"Grandma, is sex good or bad?" the kid asked.

"Ask your mother," the woman said.

Justin cracked up, wrapping Allie in his arms. "Babe, anybody who sees us together probably assumes we're going to have sex. I've got a constant semi whenever you're around. I can't believe you haven't noticed, with all the time you spend staring at my junk."

"Oh my God. Really?" She jumped in front of him and looked. "Oh my God," she repeated, turning around to walk in front of him.

"What are you doing?" he asked, grabbing her arm and yanking her to the side. "Blocking everyone's view?"

"Yes! God."

"God can see it no matter where you stand."

"You're sick. Go sit in the car. I'll go to the store alone."

"Nope." He was having too much fun tormenting her. Honestly, it was just the conversation about condoms that had him somewhat inspired. He didn't really walk around with a constant hard-on, but if it kept Allie blushing, he might have to find a way to make that happen.

They finally compromised, and Allie bought groceries while he took care of protection.

When he got outside, Allie was leaning into the back end of the Escape, her long legs bared by her short skirt, her fine ass perfectly inviting.

Unfortunately, it was a very public parking lot, so he couldn't approach her the way he wanted to and press himself against her, letting her know how glad he was to see her. Some asshole in a jacked-up Dodge Ram whistled as he passed. Allie turned to see, then gave them a dismissive wave.

Justin sneered. "Poser. Real men drive their mom's five-year-old mini SUV because we don't have to overcompensate. And we still get the best girls."

Allie responded with a smile that made his secret longing for a Ford F-250 Super Duty float away like diesel exhaust.

He backed her against the side of the car and gave her a long, hot kiss.

"Let's get back to the campground," she panted into his ear after they broke apart.

"That's my girl," he said, reaching behind her to pull open the car door.

She paused for a moment, mouth open, then snapped it shut again and gave him the smile that said she had more than dinner planned when they got back.

• • •

They finally found the campground close to the festival location. And they'd been assigned a campsite next to the world's longest, fanciest two-story RV, which was covered with a larger than large photo of Billy Bob Panko, grand-père of cheesy restaurants.

Still trying to keep her spirits up, Justin told Allie it was a sign that she had to keep trying. She told him she didn't have a choice. *Atta girl.*

Billy Bob's screen door was open and the sounds of *Wheel of Fortune* drifted from the inside.

"I'm going to go borrow some ketchup," she told Justin after they'd set up their camper—Rainbow Dog sign artfully placed where it faced the Panko-mobile—and started to pre-pare dinner on the little grill they set up on the picnic table.

"There's a bottle in the—" Justin was cut off when she gave him the universal "shut the hell up and follow my lead" look, which involved a fair amount of eye widening and lip pursing.

"Okay."

She walked over, knocked on the door of the Billy Bob Express, and when a walking, talking sixty-year-old Barbie opened it, she introduced herself and said, "My guy here for-got one of his major food groups—ketchup. I don't suppose y'all have a bottle we can borrow? I'll run into town and get another one first thing tomorrow, but we're having steak, and he just won't eat meat without drowning it," she told the woman.

Billy Bob's voice echoed throughout the campground

when he yelled from somewhere inside, "We don't have any goddamned ketchup. And even if we did, we wouldn't let your dog eat it. Get her a bottle of Billy Bob! On second thought, you two come on over here and eat with us."

Allie turned to Justin and shot him a triumphant smile. She turned back to Mrs. Billy Bob, who rolled her eyes and grinned.

Over the next two hours, Justin listened to Billy Bob explain how to cook every kind of meat from pork to partridge. Season it, smoke the hell out of it, and dump a quart of Billy Bob's on it.

The overly sweet but somehow addictively tangy sauce would ruin the flavor of the best rib eye, but Billy Bob had something going on when it came to marketing his sauce. The Panko family owned a string of a hundred restaurants between Roanoke and Tulsa, and they sold their signature barbecue sauce in grocery stores across America. They had a reality show called *Porkers*, which had a seriously dedicated viewership, or so Allie had assured Justin.

He kept waiting for the camera crews to arrive, but Mrs. Billy Bob—Maggie—confided that she'd insisted this trip was a second honeymoon for them, and no cameras were allowed in the campground. Allie seemed disappointed, no doubt looking forward to the marketing boost that a guest appearance on *Porkers* would provide.

As they finished their pulled pork sandwiches, Allie said, "I'll go get dessert. It's the least I can do, after you fed us this wonderful meal."

Justin wasn't sure how there was going to be room in his body for more food, but when he saw what Allie brought out, he managed to sit up a little straighter and find a few more inches inside. "Are those bourbon balls? Where were you hiding that?" he asked when he saw what she brought out.

She shot him a canary-eating cat smile. "I have to keep some secrets," she said. "And these are Brown Dog Balls."

"Umm…" Billy Bob stared at the plate of round chocolates.

"Well," Allie said. "Brown Dog is one of the new products we're debuting at the festival tomorrow. It's a chocolate-coffee flavored whiskey."

"I hope this tastes better than it sounds," the old man grumbled, popping one into his mouth. He chewed, swallowed, and grinned, taking two more from the plate.

Allie had her foot in the door. She explained their project, how white dog was un-aged bourbon whiskey, and how they planned to market different colored—and flavored—dogs.

Justin didn't know how she did it, but she managed to persuade Billy Bob to consider introducing Rainbow Dog drinks in his restaurants, and maybe even serving her Brown Dog "bourbon" balls on the dessert menu.

"I don't know, girl. Not sure we can call them Brown Dog Balls. Although I guess that's better than Brown Dog Turds, which is kind of what it looks like." The whole camper shook with Billy Bob's laughter.

They spent a couple of hours with the Pankos, then Justin feigned a sore ankle as an excuse to get Allie alone in their own camper.

"They're awesome, don't you think?" she asked, throwing her arms around his neck.

"I think you're awesome," he agreed, nibbling on her ear.

She giggled, but said, "It's great, but it's still not an investor. I mean, if he signs a contract, we might be able to do some creative financing, but…"

"We'll get there. It'll be fine," he said.

"I'm getting worried. I'd feel better if we were going into On the Rocks with at least a few possible leads. Then it would be easier to get someone with more cash there."

"It's gonna be fine."

Allie, whose smile was becoming more and more essential to Justin's existence, frowned. "I hope so."

"It will be." He wasn't going to tell her how he was so sure, because he really wanted her to know that it was her, without his interference. Her product, her pitch, her business sense that would seal the deal with Merilee when she showed up and offered to be a silent partner in Rainbow Dog. He was just the…matchmaker.

Chapter Twenty-Two

The day of the On the Rocks festival dawned hot and muggy, but the conference center was well air-conditioned. A good thing, because there was a lot of work to do.

By the time Allie got through the line and managed to add Rainbow Dog as a late entry to the product competitions, Justin had—with one bulging, tattooed arm—unloaded the last case of Allie's secret mugs into the booth. "I got us signed up!" she said. "We'll see soon enough if I've been wasting our time."

"Darlin'," Justin said, catching her around the waist and pulling her in for a kiss, "if we don't have this business locked down solid by the end of the weekend, I'll eat my hat. Or you. Although I'll probably eat you anyway."

She laughed and pushed him away. "I've unleashed a monster."

"Let's unleash these mugs you've been so anxious about," he said.

She opened the top box and pulled out one of the tiny mason-jar-shaped shot glasses and handed one to him.

He looked at it but didn't speak.

"What do you think?"

He shrugged and put it back in the box. "It's okay."

"Just okay?" The glasses were etched with a cartoon bulldog face that David had drawn on everything when he was in high school. The Marine Corps mascot was a bulldog, and David had made his own version, simpler and friendlier. Allie thought it was perfect for Rainbow Dog. Cute, but badass.

"Yeah, it's fine." He turned and began lining up bottles of the various flavors of Rainbow Dog on the back table.

"I thought it would be a nice thing, a way to include David in the process."

Justin straightened, fingered the watch that she'd seen him tuck into his pocket. He nodded, then met her gaze, and one side of his mouth rose. "Yeah, I like it."

Did she really think he was going to coo and gurgle over them? She took a breath and reintroduced the cemetery idea. "I think he'd like it. I was going to take him one on the way back to Crockett County."

Justin looked at her then, face blank. "What are you talking about?"

She took a deep breath. "Arlington. I want to go to Arlington on the way home."

"I don't—" A muscle ticked in his jaw.

"Fine. You can wait in the camper."

What the heck was wrong with him? She wasn't asking him to write poetry to read over the grave, just to go to the damned cemetery with her. She thought maybe he could use some closure—he hadn't stuck around after Dave's funeral and never talked about him. She'd thought that maybe with his approval of the shot glasses, he was putting that aside.

But maybe there was more. Maybe there was something he wasn't telling her.

He hadn't responded, just kept working.

"Well, we can talk about it later, I guess." He half nodded at her, a whole lot more of no response, as far as she was concerned.

Something over her shoulder caught his eye then, and his face lit up. "Hey, babe!"

He brushed past her, and she turned in time to see her lover scoop Merilee Cooper into his arms and lift her into the air. He probably would have spun his high school sweetheart in a circle if a gimpy leg and space constraints hadn't been an issue.

Something deep in Allie's chest constricted, and her extremities went numb.

But then Justin put Merilee down, turned, and pulled Allie against his side, saying, "Hey, Merilee, do you remember Allie McGrath?"

The buzzing in Allie's ears eased slightly as Merilee's smile tightened, and she nodded. "Sure do. How's it going?" She even held a hand out for Allie to shake.

Okay, so Allie was overreacting to old wounds. PTRD—post-traumatic romance disorder. But still. The bitch hadn't gotten any shorter, fatter, or less perfectly blonde.

Justin didn't release Allie as he asked, "How long are you back in the States?"

Merilee's smile really fled then. "I'm back for good. My husband…he passed away."

The devil on Allie's shoulder pointed out that Merilee was now free to pick up where she'd left off with Justin at the same time the angel was kicking Allie in the back of the head for being so selfish. Angel won for the moment. "I'm so sorry, Merilee," Allie said.

"Thank you."

She even looked beautiful when she was choked up, Devil pointed out.

"Where are you staying?" Justin asked.

Grrrr...said Devil.

"With my parents at Quail Hill for now," she told them.

"Are you going to work for their distillery?" Allie asked.

Merilee shot Justin a look that Allie couldn't interpret. "Actually, no. I'm looking to branch out in some less...traditional directions. I'm fortunate to have some options." She looked at Allie and said, "My late husband left me fairly well-off."

Angel pointed out that she shouldn't jump right on that information...the woman was no doubt still wounded from the loss of her spouse. But if she was looking for somewhere to invest an inheritance...

Devil told Angel to shut the fuck up, because Allie needed an investor, and it wasn't like she was going to suck poor Merilee into a Ponzi scheme.

"What's all this?" Merilee asked, picking up one of the bulldog shot glasses. "Is Blue Mountain going to the dogs?"

Allie laughed politely at the joke. "Not exactly. Blue Mountain has a couple of bourbons entered—one in the single-barrel category and Sean's Small Batch. And we're presenting Dangerous Dave's 8-Ball, but no booth for Blue Mountain this year." Thanks to Lorena, who had canceled their booth after learning that Allie and Justin had planned to run it next to Rainbow Dog. "The dogs are part of a new company I'm starting on my own. Rainbow Dog."

"Tell me about it."

Allie looked at Justin, and he was watching her, waiting for her to answer. She loved that he didn't try to take over. "It's a new product I entered in the innovations category. We're rolling it out here."

She explained her idea, to bottle white dog whiskey and market it to the moonshine crowd. It would be cheaper to produce than bourbon, and a fun, hip way to introduce a younger crowd to whiskey, in the hopes that they'd develop a taste and be willing to spend more on the higher-end bourbons when their income levels allowed.

"I like it. When do you start releasing it to the public?"

"It kind of depends."

"Ah," she said, nodding sagely. "The Blue Mountain old farts don't think it's a good idea, do they?"

Allie didn't answer, her condescension stinging.

Justin spoke up then. "They've got their heads up their collective ass. Allie's got her act together."

If he hadn't stolen her heart before that moment, Allie would have gone completely over the edge. As it was, she melted, just a little more, into Justin's side.

"I like it." Merilee pulled a card from somewhere and handed it to Allie. To her, not to Justin.

Merilee Cooper Gordon, CEO, Spirit Enterprises.

Both Devil and Angel nudged Allie. "I'm glad. I have some investment opportunities if you're interested in learning more."

"Let's talk later. I think I can help you out."

Allie just nodded. Would it be that easy? Would Merilee just cut her a check?

Angel and Devil crossed their arms and raised their eyebrows.

• • •

Allie was quiet after Merilee left, and Justin had a sneaking suspicion that she was having some girl-insecurity shit, but wasn't about to get into the "Are you okay?"-"I'm fine" cycle that he'd been caught in a few times and witnessed more than a few.

He didn't know if she even remembered that he'd dated Merilee back in the day. At some point, during one of his early deployments, he'd stopped emailing Merilee, and she'd eventually sent him a Dear John letter—just to tie up the loose ends.

"Hey," he said, catching Allie's hand as she passed by with a stack of business cards.

"Hey, what?" she said, swinging around to land on his lap.

He tugged her hair until she was face-to-face with him, and then he kissed her. He put every bit of you're-the-only-woman-for-me he could into it, and hoped she got the message.

"What was that for?"

Apparently not. "Because you're my girl."

She didn't smile right away, as he expected. Did she doubt him?

Or maybe she was annoyed that he was refusing to go to the cemetery to see Dave's grave. He just couldn't go there.

Maybe someday, but…

Finally her lips curved up, and she kissed him back. "I'm glad you think so," she said.

What the hell did that mean?

Someone from the liquor board came along and kept him from asking. The officials double-checked that Justin and Allie had all of the appropriate paperwork in place, and another gave them more shit to fill out for the best booth contest. Between the more formal tasting for the single-barrel bourbon, the innovative beverage category, and all the miscellaneous hoopla competitions, they were bound to win something, Justin hoped.

Finally, the doors to the conference center were opened, and people began to stream into the ballroom. Visitors bought a wristband that said they were over twenty-one, and then were allowed to buy a certain number of tickets, each of which entitled them to a miniature serving of the beverage of their choice.

Rainbow Dog's booth was in an area Blue Mountain hadn't been in before. Normally, their booth was grouped with the traditional bourbons, where most everyone truly was related to someone else, at least by marriage, and the business rivalries were put aside on the golf course, and always at the bar.

This year, they were located in a much more interesting area. Instead of horse statues and topiary, wagon wheels and rustic fence posts, the Innovative Beverage area was full of fluorescent leis and flashing lights, rap music and semi-naked spokesmodels.

"Hey, babe, why don't you have on a belly shirt like all the other liquor wenches?" Justin asked Allie, dipping his lips to her neck for one last nuzzle before the crowd and their drink tickets descended on them.

"I don't know. Why are you wearing a shirt at all?" she asked.

He started to laugh, but then decided to call her bluff. He took off his shirt, which caused the tequila shooter girls across the aisle to hoot and clap. He undid the top button of his jeans, letting them fall a little lower on his hips. He wasn't going to be sharing any butt crack with anyone, but maybe a hip dimple.

"Oh, for God's sake," Allie said. "Okay, okay. With the limp and the bruises, that might be a little too much. Maybe just go for 'hot military guy.'"

"Good idea," he answered, kissing her as he dug in his pocket and pulled out his dog tags, and put them over his head.

She rolled her eyes, and he smacked her on the ass. This was actually going to be fun, he decided.

"Hey, darlin,' what kind of dog do you like?" he asked their first visitor, an ultra-blonde middle-aged woman with either a very good plastic surgeon, or a platinum shopper card at Victoria's Secret.

She eyed Justin, and said, "You look like a sporting breed."

Allie leaned toward the woman and said, "He sheds and won't stay off the furniture. I suggest you try the Red Dog. That one's at least housebroken." She handed the woman one of her little shot glasses with a splash of Red Dog.

The woman took a small sip, then tilted her head back and shot the rest. "Damn!" she said, tapping her chest, which didn't make her breasts move at all. "Honey, you gotta try this!"

She yanked on the sleeve of an enormous black man, who turned to the booth with a smile.

"Holy shit," Justin whispered. "That's Lyle Doggens."

Allie looked at the man, who smiled and nodded at Justin, acknowledging he'd been recognized. She had the sense to wait until the couple walked away, admiring the shot glasses, before asking Justin to tell her who Lyle Doggens was.

"Only the greatest football player in the history of the Atlanta Falcons. He's part owner now."

"Uh-huh," she said.

Their next guest wore a flannel plaid shirt with the sleeves cut off, and a John Deere hat that had absorbed more than its recommended lifetime allowance of sweat.

At one point, she dug her phone out of her pocket and looked at it. "Huh," she said, and shoved it back into her pants.

"What's wrong?" he asked.

"Nothing. That's Eve. They're still coming, but said they got held up. Maybe Brandon got Montezuma's revenge or something. They'll be here tomorrow."

Justin shrugged. Brandon and Eve were originally supposed to meet the distillery managers here for the awards ceremony while the old folks rested up from the cruise, but now that he and Allie were here, they could accept awards for both Blue Mountain bourbon *and* Rainbow Dog whiskey if need be.

As she handed another customer a shot glass with some Green Dog in it, telling him it was better than an apple a day, he watched her work the crowd.

She turned and smiled her special Allie smile at him, and… Fuck. He was in so much trouble.

Chapter Twenty-Three

By the time the opening night closed, Allie and Justin had given away every shot glass, and had resorted to giving away unused labels as free stickers—and had an impromptu drawing for the empty jars. Everyone loved all the colors of Rainbow Dog. The Dog was *big*.

"Do we have enough product for tomorrow?" Justin asked as they gathered the empty boxes and tossed them in a pile for the cleanup crew.

Allie grinned. "I think so. But I'm gonna have to find a twenty-four-hour printer for more labels, and make a run to the party outlet for shot glasses." Maybe she'd talk to Billy Bob about carrying Rainbow Dog mugs or something when they introduced the drinks. Like going to Pat O'Brien's in New Orleans and getting a fancy glass with each different kind of drink.

She felt pretty damned good about things. One of the judges had stopped to have a taste, and Allie noticed that he came back an hour later with a friend. Billy Bob and Maggie had been by, and when they couldn't get close to the booth, Maggie shot Allie a thumbs-up and a wink.

She was finally starting to see evidence that what she believed was true: she knew what she was doing.

And she wasn't even that worried that Merilee had shown her perfect self up to stir the pot of Allie's anxiety stew. Justin was with her, and she was his Ms. Right Now. And, her crazy heart pointed out, until he got on that plane, he hadn't left. Who knew if he'd really go?

Justin threw the last box over the side of the booth and flopped onto a folding chair.

"How are you holding up?" she asked. He'd been on that leg for four hours straight, which was probably a little longer than the doctor had meant when he said he could use the walking boot as much as he was comfortable.

He pulled her down onto his good knee and nuzzled her neck. That knee was fast becoming her favorite seat. "I'm holding you up just fine. What else do we have to do here?"

She looked around. "I guess just check out with the organizer. We don't have any liquor to return."

They said good-bye to a few other vendors and made their way to the exit. Justin was definitely limping. "Okay," she told him. "You've got to wait here. I'll go get the car."

"I can make it," he said. "Besides, you're not walking through a dark parking garage alone."

It was a little creepy, but all of the drunken guests had left hours ago.

"I'll walk with you." Merilee appeared from nowhere. "You can drop me at my car after we get to yours."

Yay. More chances to make nice. Allie turned to Justin

and pressed her body to his, tilting her face up for a kiss. Her lips against his, she said, "Stay here. You need to conserve some energy."

He gave a low groan and kissed her. "Go get the car."

When the door to the stairwell closed behind them, Merilee said, "So. You and Justin are a couple now?"

"Um, yeah." Allie didn't know what else to say.

"I guess you could have been together a long time ago, if I hadn't elbowed you out of the way."

Allie stopped in her tracks, staring at Merilee. Son of a bitch. All these years she'd thought Merilee had ruined her chances with him, but really? She'd cost her some self-esteem and a lot of ice cream, but what would have happened if she hadn't been there? Allie'd have thrown herself at Justin, embarrassed them both, and nothing would have changed, except it probably would have been worse.

"Are you okay?" Merilee asked. "You look like you've seen a ghost."

"Yeah. I'm fine." But she did need to find a way to move the conversation from past hurt feelings to current business opportunities. She clicked the remote for Justin's mom's SUV and it beeped from the next row. "There it is. I'm glad you walked up here with me. Can I drop you at your car?"

"Nah. I'm right over there." She waved at a little sports car.

"Will you be here for the rest of the weekend? Maybe we can have coffee before things get started tomorrow." Allie cringed to hear how false she sounded. Coffee with Merilee? If Eve got here in time for that, she'd laugh her ass off.

But Merilee shook her head. "Let's talk now. I really am

impressed with your Rainbow Dog. I know you're looking for an investor, but I'm looking for a little more." She handed Allie a sheet of paper.

Talk about prepared! At first, it was just a series of columns of numbers, but then it slowly began to make sense. Production estimates, sales projections, income potential. Holy crap, had the woman been sitting with her laptop doing math since she'd visited the booth earlier? Allie's scalp tingled with anticipation. This was it, her investor, her silent partner, her proof that she could pull it off!

"I'd like to buy the brand. You're welcome to stay on in some capacity, and I'm going to ask Justin to oversee production management."

The speculative look in Merilee's eye drove the words home and sent a spike of nausea through Allie. For an instant, she was standing in an airport arrival zone, holding a poster with her hopes and dreams out in public.

"I know." Merilee laughed. "I'm a little surprised, too. But it's an awesome product. What do you think? Want to sell it to me?"

Allie zoomed back into the here and now. The blonde blocking her way might try to grab her soldier, but she didn't have him yet. And this time, Merilee wouldn't get Allie's dignity, or anything else. "I'm not going to sell the brand. I'm gonna own the company myself. I'd love an investor—a silent investor who'll get a healthy rate of return—but it's still going to be my business. Can you reconsider?"

Merilee scrunched her face for a moment, then said, "Nope. I want it all. But you think about it, okay?"

Before she got in the SUV, Allie said she'd keep the offer in mind—but only because she didn't know how she could forget it.

Things had gone so well that evening that she felt really confident that an investor would come along, and everything would be just fine.

• • •

Allie took a moment to appreciate the pine forest that surrounded the long drive into the campground. Whatever happened, right now it was still all good.

"Are you okay?" Justin asked. "You're awfully quiet. What did Merilee have to say on your walk to the garage?"

She didn't want to wreck the evening by telling him that the evil queen was still interested in him, so she just said, "I'm still processing. Nothing there we can take to the bank at the moment."

"Really." He sounded surprised.

A few yards inside the entrance to the camping area, a doe meandered out of the pitch-black night onto the road, its eyes glowing in the headlights. Allie, already driving slowly, hit the brakes until it decided to move along, up a little gravel side road that led to the parking area for a hiking trail. A buck followed without even glancing their way.

"He thinks he's gonna get lucky." Justin's chuckle stroked over Allie's skin. She was that sensitized, that tuned into his frequencies—every sound and motion, every glance, sent hormones coursing through her body.

She looked at Justin, and back at the road where the deer had gone. Then she turned and looked at the rear seat of the SUV. "You know, we haven't done it in a car yet."

"Allie, the camper's just about a quarter of a mile farther

up the road," he said as she turned onto the little gravel road up to a picnic area at a trailhead.

She shot him a smile. "Bucket list. I'm starting one right now. This is on it."

"Oh, Jesus." He shifted in his seat.

She looked, and by the dashboard light she saw paradise trying to shove its way out of Justin's jeans.

She tucked the SUV as far back in a corner of the parking lot as she could.

"Aren't you worried that the psycho killer with the hook hand is going to show up?"

She unbuckled her seatbelt. "I have the greatest recruit in the history of the Marine Corps here to protect me," she said.

"I have a feeling I'm going to be a little distracted," Justin said.

"Race you to the backseat," she said.

It took a couple of minutes to find the flippy thing to lay the seat flat, and by the time they scrambled into the back end of the car, both were laughing, and the urgency of the moment had passed.

But then Justin pulled Allie down next to him and turned on his side, facing her, with his head resting on his fist.

"I'm glad you blackmailed me into coming on this trip," he said, tracing the line of the arm she'd slung over his waist and making her shiver.

"And I'm glad you're a bleeding heart who donated all of your savings to Operation Homefront, so you needed money."

He jerked, his surprise evident. "How did you know?"

She shrugged. "I saw the thank-you note."

He leaned a little closer, and she felt his warm breath against the top of her head. "I've got a feeling you already know all my secrets."

"Uh-huh," she said. She stroked her hand up his side, then back down, sliding under his shirt, feeling him quiver at her touch.

"So you should probably tell me one of yours," he said, running his teeth along her neck.

He didn't need to know what a fool she'd been when she was younger, but she could give him this much. It was the partial truth. "I had a sex dream about you in high school."

He groaned. "You didn't."

She laughed. "Are you shocked?"

"I feel kind of dirty."

"Want to hear it?"

"Hells yeah!"

"It's kind of lame. You came home on leave, and we went on a date."

"Really?" He pulled back and looked at her. "Tell me more."

"Dinner and a movie."

"What did we see?"

"I don't remember?"

"Well, then, where did we eat?"

"Do you want to get to the good stuff, or not?"

"Fine. But if I'd been away, I'd have liked to go to Big Buds, down on Beaver Road."

"Okay, then that's where we went. But then afterward, we took a drive down Ripple Run." Where everyone from Crockett County went to make out. "Then, when you stopped the car, you did the old movie theater yawn and reach, so you could get your arm around me."

"I bet I made up constellations to point out to you so you had to lean your head closer to mine to see through the windshield."

He pulled her close, tilted her face up to his. In the darkness she felt his breath stutter, the coiled tension under his hot skin.

"What constellations?" Whatever her dream had been about fled under this new, better, shared one.

"You know. The usual. Copulous Major, and Vaginus Minor."

Snorting, she asked, "And then how would you get me to kiss you?"

"I'm pretty sure that at that point, you'd have been all over me," he said, leaning back and pulling her with him.

And so she was. She bent to kiss him and licked between his lips, met by his tongue, stroking and licking. She gasped as he nipped at her lower lip and then soothed it with his tongue, sucking it into his mouth and letting go.

She was restless, her lower body arching toward his, and she moved her legs so that one of his was between hers. She pressed her aching core against his hard thigh, running her hands over his chest, toying with his nipples through the soft cotton of the T-shirt as he groaned.

"I think I probably needed to explore you," she said. "I was dying for you to feel me up, see if a big, experienced man was any better at it than—"

"I don't want to know," he growled, and didn't that just make her clench a little bit around his thigh.

"But I was too anxious to see what you looked like under your uniform." She sat up and straddled him, stroking herself against his erection through the layers of clothing between them. She pushed up his shirt while he lay back, arms behind his head, watching through glittering eyes.

She stroked down his chest, from his collarbone, over his pecs, pausing at his nipples, leaning in to take each one in her mouth for a moment, loving the little helpless sounds he made. Then she moved to the center of his chest, kissing the place where his ribs met, moving lower.

"Oh, hell," he muttered.

"I'd never been this far with a guy before," she said, running her fingers through the line of hair leading to his waistband, kissing his belly button, reaching for the button on his jeans. "Oh, my," she said, pressing down on the hard line of his cock, finding the contours through denim.

She was drunk with arousal, completely focused on his body, imagining them ten years ago, but right there, right now, with him in her hands.

Unzipping his jeans, she pushed the fabric out the way and freed his erection, hearing him sigh as she stroked him, loving the feel of silky skin stretched over hard flesh. She moved back, scooting down his legs, pulling his jeans to the top of his brace.

Then she had room to work. She leaned down, nuzzling him, breathing in the musky scent of his body, feeling the way his stomach quivered when she spoke. "I was a little nervous about this part, because if I messed it up, you'd know what a novice I was. But did it anyway." She licked him then, loving the taste of his arousal and the way he felt against her lips. She took him into her mouth, sliding him as deep as she could.

"I'm pretty sure you couldn't mess this up," he said.

"Jesus. Just seeing you there now—there's no way I could have—" He moaned when she sucked and then stroked his balls, feeling them pull up toward his body. "Dammit, Allie, I'm close. And it's your turn. If you don't want—"

In answer, she sucked harder, holding him steady as she moved over him, trying not to pull back when he hit the back of her throat, but not caring, just wanting to have him.

"Oh, fuck!" Justin said. He was coming. Pulses jetted into her mouth, but then he was pulling away from her, telling her to stop.

She sat back, gasping, shocked, just as headlights swept the interior of the car.

"Oh, shit." She scrambled to help him pull himself together while turning around to...what? Try to look like they weren't doing what they were doing?

She peered through the window, making out the strip of lights on the top of the pickup truck that was now stopped a few yards from their car.

She turned to Justin, who'd managed to get his pants up and zipped. "What should we do?"

He shrugged. "Believe it or not, I've never been in this position," he told her.

"Never had sex in the back of a car?"

"Never been *busted* having sex in the back of a car."

She laughed. "Well. At least that's something I can say I have more experience with than you."

He waved his hands in front of his face. "No, don't want to know!"

He was determined not to know about other guys in her life. That made her feel pretty damned good. She'd wanted him for as long as she could remember; it was an amazing feeling to know he wanted her, too. For however long it lasted.

"Okay, well, I think we should get out."

They both opened the doors on their respective sides of the car. The truck was parked on Allie's side, so it was her face the park ranger hit first with the beam of his flashlight. He started to move it away and then came back to her, making her blink. Then he shone the light on Justin before aiming it out of their eyes.

"You folks realize the park is closed after dark?" he said.

"Um, sorry, sir," Allie said. "We're staying at the campground. We just, uh, saw a deer come up this way and we followed it..."

"Um, yeah," Justin offered, ever the helpful one. "To the backseat."

Chapter Twenty-Four

By the time the emcee for the taste awards announced the Best New Product category, Allie had chewed off every fingernail she had and was eyeing Justin's hands. Unfortunately, his nails were already trimmed down to the quick.

"Here. Have some gum." Justin handed her a pack of Juicy Fruit, and she tore into a piece, then carefully folded the wrapper and slid it under her plate. They'd gotten word when they arrived that morning that both Blue Mountain and Rainbow Dog had finaled in a couple of categories. Allie was through the roof.

She wished Eve and Brandon would get here. They were supposed to come today while the older folks recovered from the cruise. At any rate, they would bear witness to her mother that she'd done something right.

"Our last award before we have a brief intermission is the Best New Product for 2015," the announcer said. Then images of each of the finalists were flashed on the screen behind the podium. Rainbow Dog was competing against a classic Kentucky bourbon; a vodka from, of all places, Mexico; and a rum. "And the best new product for 2015 isn't even on the market yet. Blue Mountain's Rainbow Dog!"

Allie and Justin looked at each other in shock, then he stood up and pulled her to her feet, lifting her in the air and spinning her in an enthusiastic, if somewhat staggering, circle. As everyone clapped and cheered, he kissed her and dragged her toward the podium.

He accepted the giant ice-cube-shaped trophy and pushed Allie toward the microphone.

"Um..." she said, at a loss for words for probably the first time in her life. "I don't know quite what to say."

She looked at Justin, but he wasn't going to help her.

Turning back to the audience, she said, simply, "I had this idea, and I told the family about it, but they all kind of patted me on the head and sent me on my way."

The audience tittered.

"I told my brother, David, about it, in an email while he was serving in Afghanistan. And he wrote back and said, 'Sneezy, it's not what I would do, but I wouldn't wear lipstick, either, and that seems to work for you.'"

The crowd laughed.

She sobered then and looked around for Justin. She grabbed his hand and continued. "David died a few days later, when his unit came under fire." The audience was silent now. Justin squeezed her hand. She was grateful that he was with her or she probably wouldn't have been able to talk at all.

"I think most of my family would say that I've always been all guts and not enough rational thought, but I'm glad

I listened to my intuition about Rainbow Dog and I think David would have been proud of me. Thanks."

To the sound of applause, she moved aside to give Justin a shot at the microphone, but he shook his head. "It's all yours, babe," he said.

When the ceremony broke up for an intermission as they returned to their table, Allie and Justin were surrounded by well-wishers, although he pushed all the questions her way.

But then he looked over her shoulder and said, "Don't look now, but it's about to be family hour."

She whipped her head around so fast she'd have a sore neck later. Sure enough, there was Lorena, followed by Eve a few paces behind. Her sister shot her a glance, but even with that advance warning, her mother's gracious smile, her even, ladylike pace, her steady gaze, all screamed "Danger, Mommy's pissed" to her daughters.

No one else but Allie and Eve would have called it, but there was a storm brewing. Her stomach clenched, a wave of anxiety coating her insides.

Lorena nodded to Allie, and then, almost as an afterthought, to Justin, as she pulled out her chair and sat. She crossed her elegant legs and turned the coffee cup at her place upright, and a waiter filled it immediately, as though he'd followed her from the door. He probably had.

The awards ceremony started again before she had a chance to speak to her mom, and Allie clapped politely when everyone else did, but didn't really pay too much attention to who won what.

She had a big chance to make her name and launch Rainbow Dog, but how much rain was Lorena going to dump on her parade? Justin took her hand on the other side of the table, under the cover of the tablecloth, and rubbed his thumb over her knuckles, soothing her and yet making her hyperaware of how much her hands were sweating.

When the waiter held the coffee carafe up in a silent question, she shook her head no. Even decaf would send her heart rate into the danger zone right now. She had a bad, bad feeling.

The nominees for small batch bourbon of the year were announced, and Allie sat up, smiling along with her mother, Eve, and Justin. "And the winner is, another entry from Blue Mountain Bourbon—Sean McGrath's Small Batch."

Lorena's smile was frozen for only an instant, but it was enough for Allie to realize that she'd caught the "another entry" comment from the announcer. As far as Lorena knew, the only entry should have been Sean's Small Batch. Bad enough Allie had brought Rainbow Dog for people to taste. But to dare put it in the competition? The shit was about to hit the fan.

• • •

After the awards were distributed and the final thank-yous were said, Justin followed the McGraths to the lobby for a press conference.

They posed for a couple of photos for trade magazines and Kentucky news websites, and then a reporter asked Lorena the question of the day. "Blue Mountain Distilling has always been such a traditional bourbon-only distillery. What made you all decide to take the leap into the world of trendy drinks?"

Lorena laughed, and if Justin didn't know better, he'd

think Allie's mother didn't have a care in the world. Unfortunately, Lorena could camouflage her anger and bring it out when one was least expecting it. Eve stepped back, eyes wide in alarm. "Well, it's all been an interesting experiment, hasn't it? You can be certain that the quality and tradition that Blue Mountain represents will be always first and foremost when you see the Blue Mountain name on a label."

Ouch. Allie flinched, just barely, but it was enough that he noticed and pulled her close. Lorena didn't miss that, either. With the barest of raised eyebrows, she looked at him and turned away. Had he just been warned?

Finally, the damned party was over and they were able to leave. Justin gathered a copy of the program and the Rainbow Dog trophy, while Eve picked up the one for the Sean McGrath.

The original plan had been for Allie and Eve to get ready for the fancy-ass dance while Justin and Brandon waited in the bar, but Brandon was nowhere to be seen. Repeated texts had gone unanswered.

"Why didn't Brandon come?" he asked Eve.

"I don't know," Eve said. "Brandon jumped ship in Puerta Feo. And your folks went back to Blue Mountain to check on things."

If the look on Allie's face reflected surprise, his own must have been the Google Images result for *Shock and Awe*. Brandon didn't "jump ship." Ever.

He pulled out his phone again—he'd have to actually call. "Hey, I'm going to try to reach him. Can I catch up with you in a few?"

"Sure. We're gonna go to get Eve checked into her room now, okay?"

He nodded and limped toward the bar. Before he called Brandon, he texted Merilee. Allie still hadn't told him what went down between them last night, and he was itching to find out.

Did you offer to invest in Rainbow?

It only took a moment for her reply.

Not exactly. Can you meet to talk about alternatives?

Huh? What alternatives?

Allie's busy right now. What time?

Not with Allie, just want to talk to you.

What the hell? Not his decision. At all. But he supposed he'd better talk to her, find out what she had up her sleeve.

He pulled out a barstool and thought about ordering a drink. He'd been sober for over a week now, but today seemed like a good day to break the habit.

"Justin." He looked up to see Lorena bearing down on him. "I think we need to have a talk."

"What can I get you?" asked the bartender, putting a coaster and a bowl of peanuts on the bar.

"Double shot of Cuervo Gold," he said. If they'd had Rainbow Dog, he'd have ordered a pint.

"Tequila?" Lorena asked, raising an eyebrow. To the bartender, she said, "Club soda with a lime."

"What can I do for you, Lorena?" Justin said. Funny. He'd never harbored animosity toward Allie's mother before, even though he suspected she blamed him for Dave's enlistment. Truth be told, it had been Dave's idea. Justin had been bitching about his dad, about how much he didn't want to work at Blue Mountain just because it was expected of him, and Dave had said, "So let's do something else for a while. Something useful."

Lorena had thrown a fit—in the way only Lorena could. She completely shut down. Not that Justin blamed her. Dave's dad had just died of self-inflicted drunk driving, leaving the distillery on rocky financial ground—that they were only just now digging out of—and then her only son was about to dive headfirst into a war that appeared like it might never end.

Justin felt sorry for Lorena. But he was protective of Allie, who wanted her mother's approval more than she realized. Probably more than she wanted Rainbow Dog off the ground.

"What do you think you two are doing?"

He didn't pretend not to know what she was talking about. "We'd drop-kick Blue Mountain into the future, if you'd let us. As it is, we're going to get there on our own." And they would. Even if Merilee had pulled a fast one and bailed—he was going to find out what was going on.

But Lorena was still at it. "With that—that—*moonshine*?"

He picked up his shot of tequila. "Rainbow Dog is hardly backwoods hooch. It's good Blue Mountain white dog."

"But Blue Mountain doesn't sell anything younger than seven years old. This is a convention we've followed for as long as we've been in business. And even if we decided to release something younger, we certainly wouldn't let it be anything that couldn't be called Kentucky straight bourbon whiskey. I'm surprised you've let her talk you into this. And

David would have—"

He wasn't going to play this game. "Dave was a big fan of the good old bourbons, but this is totally different."

"That's exactly my point," Lorena said. "David wanted Allie and Eve to carry on the McGrath traditions, which is why he left his life insurance to them. Allie is using it to fund this ridiculous enterprise."

The air left his chest in a rush. He realized he'd actually clenched his fist to his sternum. She'd used Dave's life insurance to cover the deductible? What had she said when he'd asked her about it? She'd been saving for a while, she'd told him. He thought she'd meant she'd been saving money that her dad had left.

Lorena looked at Justin in triumph. "You didn't know that? It wasn't enough to drag him off to that godforsaken country and get him killed?"

The accusation from Lorena cut him deeper than she could possibly know.

Chapter Twenty-Five

After Lorena left, Justin moved to a booth in the bar so he could stare into his drink in peace.

So what if Allie had lent him Dave's life insurance money instead of her dad's proceeds? It made sense that she probably used her dad's money to pay for college. Did it really matter where the money came from? He still needed to pay it back. Another debt he owed Dave…

"You look about a million miles away."

Justin looked up at Merilee standing next to his booth.

He scooted over. "Have a seat."

She laughed. "I'll leave if Allie shows up." But she sat too close.

"Oh. I wasn't really worried about that," he lied.

"Maybe you should be. She's a little scary." Merilee fake shivered, making her breasts shimmy.

"She's something, isn't she?" He smiled, in spite of his annoyance with her for keeping the truth about Dave's money from him. "Who knew she'd grow up to be so damned perfect for me?"

"What were you thinking about so deep and heavy there?" Merilee asked.

"Actually, I want to know what we need to do to convince you to invest in Rainbow Dog."

"I don't want to invest. I want you to talk her into letting me buy it. And then I want you to come and run it for me."

He reconsidered his plan to just watch the liquor roll around in the glass and thought about downing it. "Huh? No. That's not the plan. This is Allie's project. And I wouldn't do that to her, even if I thought it was a good idea. She'd be devastated."

Merilee shrugged. "She's tough. She'll recover." She put her hand on Justin's arm. She seemed a little desperate, still beautiful, but somehow…brittle.

"I saw you and thought about how life was back here, and what could have been… Why can't it still be what could have been? What if we'd stayed together, stayed in the distillery business? We could do that now…"

Oh, hell. She was trying to get him to bail on Allie and stay in the booze business. There was no way he would hurt her that way.

"Hey, I'm flattered," he told her, taking her hand off his arm and holding it.

She clutched at his fingers, smiling ruefully. "That's what I thought. Thanks but no thanks, right?"

"Something like that." He was glad this wasn't going to be painful and messy.

"Well, I should get going. No hard feelings, huh?"

"That's my girl," he said, winking at her.

"I'm going to miss you when you go out West to do your smoke-jumper thing."

He thought for a moment, about home, and Allie, and his options, and said, "You might not miss me too much."

Merilee looked up then, and her eyes widened at something over his shoulder.

He turned and saw Allie leaving the bar. As she ran around the corner, he saw just enough of her face to identify tears.

• • •

Allie almost got out of the camper and on the road before Justin arrived. She suspected Merilee had seen her escape from the bar, but wasn't sure until now.

Justin slammed through the door. "That cab ride cost me thirty-six dollars," he ground out. "What. The. Fuck."

"You're kidding, right?" Allie stopped shoving clothes into her overnight bag and picked up her ancient backpack, grabbing toiletries and dumping them in.

"You left me at the fucking hotel. That takes a lot of nerve!"

Allie stepped out of the tiny bathroom and glared at him. "I can't believe Merilee didn't give you a ride. In her hotel room."

He laughed, a harsh, bitter sound. "You've got to be kidding. Do you really think I would jump from your bed to hers?" He almost looked hurt. "What would make you think that?"

Allie remembered how he'd looked holding hands with his old lover. And how he'd sounded. *That's my girl.* How many times had he said that to her? She'd managed to block out the generic expression somehow, convinced herself that she was special, but clearly she had been wrong.

You might not have to miss me too much. God, it sounded like he was going to invite Merilee to visit him in Firestud Training Camp. He'd never even mentioned the possibility to Allie. With Allie, it had all been, *I can't stay here.*

She bit her cheek to keep from bursting into tears. "I've made a mistake. I'm sorry. I didn't realize you still had feelings for her." Made a mistake by letting her heart lead her right back into being in love with him. Yes, she was in love with him, despite how hard she'd tried to keep her distance.

"Huh?"

"I saw you holding hands with her!"

"I was trying to figure out why she changed her mind about offering to invest in Rainbow Dog! I didn't realize she thought I'd called her because I wanted to get back together."

Allie's brain squealed to a stop and shifted into low gear, turned, and began to gather speed again. "What did you do?"

"Shit. I…" He scratched through the stubble on top of his head. "I heard she was doing the venture capital thing. I called to ask her to come talk to you. Tried to call in a favor for old times' sake, but I didn't realize she'd take it the wrong way."

The last weeks of *I believe in you, Allie… Keep your chin up, Allie… You can do it, Allie…* That was all complete and utter bullshit, wasn't it? "You tried to set me up with an investor."

"Yeah."

"Because stupid little Allie can't do shit on her own."

"No—"

"You can't be my lemonade stand hero anymore, Justin. Yes, you were my hero then, when you hung out with me and helped me with all of those crazy projects, but even then, I knew those were kid things, it wasn't real! This—Rainbow Dog—this is the real deal! At least—it was—to me."

"I know it is, babe."

"Then why did you think you needed to put in the fix for me?"

"Because I promised Dave I would help you, goddammit!"

"Dave—" Her voice sounded so small, she stopped and cleared her throat, tried again, but it was no good. "Dave didn't believe in me either?"

His silence was answer enough.

"Okay." She picked up her backpack and started to sling it over her shoulder, but forgot that the zipper had broken sometime in 2008. Everything spilled to the floor.

He moved then, reached for her. "No. Allie. You've got it wrong."

"I don't think so." She stepped around him and grabbed for her wallet and keys.

"Where are you going? You can't just leave."

"Yeah, I think it's time. You can get this beast home when you're ready, right? I'll clean the rest of this shit up when you get the camper back to Blue Mountain. I'm taking your mom's car."

He was red-faced and sweating, so beautiful in his stupid desperation to be her hero—for Dave—that she was tempted to stay. But she wouldn't. Couldn't.

"What about Rainbow Dog? We've got a chance to woo

a lot of people tonight, and I'm sure you'll find an investor."

"Don't you worry about that, Justin. Your debt to my *dead* brother is cleared, and I've got an ace up my sleeve. You don't have to stay around Blue Mountain one moment after the doctor clears you for takeoff."

"That's not what—"

She closed the door behind her and stumbled down the stairs.

Her eyes blurred as she tore out of the parking area, but she wasn't crying. It was the pollen from those stupid pine trees.

Chapter Twenty-Six

Justin's shoulders slumped. How had things gone so wrong? He slammed the door shut and clunked to the bed in the back room, which was still strewn with the contents of her malfunctioning backpack.

After everything they'd become to each other, how could she just leave like that?

He took his phone from his pocket and thought about calling to say…what, exactly? To beg her to come back? So she could accuse him of not believing in her? Or wreck her memory of her brother by making her think Dave didn't have faith in her? *Fuck*. Way to go, dickhead. The one person in her family who had completely, wholeheartedly trusted Allie had just been tarnished, because Justin hadn't been able to find the right words to explain things.

Well, maybe it was for the best. He'd believed all along, until the last few crazy, sex-soaked days, that he needed to stay away from Allie for her sake, if not for his own. He'd just proven that again.

He started to pick up the things she'd dropped on her way out. If he didn't keep busy, he'd find himself in a bourbon-soaked nightmare before he knew it.

There was a notebook with a well-abused cover lying on the floor. He picked it up and flipped the pages idly, looking for inspiration in the scribbled notes inside.

The date at the top of a page caught his attention. What was this? There was a piece of computer paper taped to one page, and Justin recognized his own email address as the sender. It was dated eight years ago.

"Hey, Babe;

Thanks for the goodies. The guys think I'm the shit with a sweet young thing sending me stuff, along with such sweet notes. They're all jealous.

Be my girl and don't stop! Can't wait to see you when I get home next month."

Oh, fuck.

She'd embellished the page with little hearts all over the place, and the opposite page had all kinds of girlie shit like, "Squee!" and "OMG, I'm soooo in love!" written all over it.

Babe. Be my girl.

And then, a few pages later...

He'd had no fucking idea. He'd broken her teenage heart and hadn't even known it was in his zone.

But Merilee had known about this crush. Seeing her with Justin, and hearing him use those bullshit force-of-habit terms… No wonder Allie'd jumped to conclusions.

Maybe he should just let her go.

She was wrong about Merilee. He liked Mer, but that attraction was long past. He was in love with Allie McGrath. He didn't know how it had crept up on him so fast—probably because his defenses were down. But she'd sneaked over his fence and captured his heart.

And driven off with it into the night.

Because she was right about something. He hadn't let Dave go. He was afraid to let go of the guilt. It had defined him for so long it was part of him.

It was probably good that she'd left. She'd be bummed out for a while. She might not ever forgive him. But that was better, wasn't it? Her anger would protect her, keep her from letting his sorry ass back into her bed, from trying to save him.

God, the way she looked at him, the way her kiss, her hands on his body, everything about her brought him out of his own mind—he had so many fucked-up things swirling around in his head all the time, so many mistakes he couldn't let go of. He wanted her, wanted to let her take away the rotten parts of himself.

When he got home, he'd make reservations to get out West, out of Allie's sight so she didn't have to deal with him.

As he lay back on the clean sheets and stretched out with his hands behind his head, he thought about that last night with Dave. How one lazy, selfish decision on Justin's part had cost his best friend his life.

He closed his eyes, replaying that night—the explosion, the blood, the pain and fear on Dave's face. His own panic, and his attempts to reassure his best friend that he was going to be okay, even though there was nothing but blood and gore where Dave's legs had once been. "Hang in there, you're going to be fine. You're okay." He'd repeated it over and over, even after it was clear that his best friend was gone, after they'd dragged Justin away from Dave's body.

But as he drifted into sleep, he could swear he heard Dave's voice. "Jesus Christ, Justin. I am fine now. You were right. I'm okay. Now it's your turn."

Justin sat up, gasping, sweat pouring from his skin. What was he doing?

He'd planned to leave Crockett County for as long as he could remember because—he just had. He and his dad had always fought over everything, while his dad and Brandon worked together like two perfect cogs. Their mother said it was because Justin and his dad were so much alike. As the younger stallion, Justin planned to leave the herd, but Clyde expected him to work for the distillery and stay forever. Which just made Justin that much more determined to leave.

But did he really hate the business? He thought about the whiskey he and Dave had made, the bourbon that was now called 8-Ball. They'd had a blast with that. And even before they were old enough to drink—the summers he'd worked in the bottling plant, putting on labels, filling cases of liquor, loading trucks. Helping little Allie McGrath earn spending money by holding a *horse wash*, for crying out loud. He had friends here, people who loved him, whom he loved. Memories. Good memories. More good than bad.

Would his life be better if he left? He'd be a stranger in a strange land if he left.

And he wouldn't have Allie.

He grabbed his phone from the charger and checked to make sure it wasn't too early. When his call was answered, he said, "Hey, Dad?" And for the first time in years, Justin told his dad everything. And his dad listened.

• • •

Allie had breakfast at a Waffle House outside Greensboro. She tried to do an old-fashioned newspaper crossword puzzle, just to have something to do besides looking lonely, but apparently failed.

"You okay, honey?" The gravel-voiced middle-aged waitress asked as she filled her coffee. "You look like you need a tall stack of chocolate chip pancakes."

Why couldn't she have gotten the younger waitress with the bad dye job and the bad attitude? She wasn't up for a *nice* server.

"Just a long night, long drive ahead of me."

"Where you headed?"

"Virginia."

"Big state." The woman smiled, kindly, recognizing that Allie didn't want to talk, but giving her a chance to change her mind.

What the hell. "I'm going to Arlington. My brother's buried there."

"Oh, honey, I'm so sorry." She sat across from Allie. "Lena!" she hollered at the other server. "Come get this carafe. I'm taking my break."

After Lena stomped over and snatched the coffee urn, Allie's new friend said, "Iraq?"

"Afghanistan." And along with the syrup on her

pancakes, poured out the story of her family, her brother, her lover…

"He's in love with you, sweetheart," the older woman said finally.

"I don't think so." Allie pushed the last few bites of food around on her plate. "But even if that were true, he's leaving. He's always said so. He doesn't want to stay at Blue Mountain. And there's still the small matter of a few thousand dollars I need to come up with so he doesn't have to stay."

"I'd say that's his problem. His half of the accident and all."

"Yeah, I know, but…" Her heart clenched at the idea of Justin staying, of having to see him on a regular basis, knowing he was stuck there because she wasn't able to get her business off the ground. She'd resent her business, he'd resent her, they would both resent anyone the other person ever dated…

"Nope," she said. "It's time to cut my losses and move on."

• • •

Justin drove for several hours before stopping and making a few more phone calls and talking to his dad again.

While whistling to a song on the radio, he thought about his new job. He and his dad would butt heads now and then, but he felt good about it. He was skilled at getting stuff from one place to another, at making sure things ran smoothly. Well, as long as he didn't count the whole Allie situation. He sighed. That one was going to be harder to fix. Hopefully, it wouldn't take him as long to make up with her as it had with his dad.

His phone rang, and he almost ignored it, planning to wait until the next rest area to listen to the voicemail, but something made him pick up.

"Justin, it's Lorena McGrath."

Oh, no. "Hey, Lorena," he said. "Has something happened to Allie?"

"You could say that."

Justin's heart stopped.

"She called our lawyers today. Told them to sell her shares of Blue Mountain stock. Said something about not wanting *you* to feel obligated to her for any promises made on anyone else's behalf."

"Lorena, I have to go," he said.

He threw the phone onto the other seat and hit the gas, skipping the next two rest areas.

Chapter Twenty-Seven

Arlington National Cemetery on a late April day was a different animal from that cold, rainy February when David had been interred. There were trees blooming all over the place...were those cherry trees? Or was that only on the mall in DC? There were also people everywhere. School groups, tour buses filled the parking area to overflowing. It was such a *lively* place.

Allie checked the map, making sure she could find David's grave. She hadn't thought she would ever forget the location, but once she set off along the path toward the quadrant where he was buried, she was completely overwhelmed at the sheer number and sameness of the rows and rows of markers. It was a place to appreciate how damned lucky she was, how safe, protected by the sacrifices of so many.

The sight of all those tombstones made her family's loss both easier and worse. So many other families torn apart by this war and all of the others that had come before—and would no doubt come after. There was comfort in knowing she wasn't alone in her pain, but also frustrated that the world couldn't seem to turn without conflict.

She found the section and walked along the row of markers, taking her time to read the punctuation of other lives, the births and deaths of all the other warriors and their family members—because their contribution to the military couldn't be overlooked. Even though she felt like she didn't do anything but sit at home while David and Justin put their boots on and fought, she supposed that her emails and care packages counted for something. She only wished the pain she felt could be quantified and redirected into the hearts of the people who'd killed her brother.

Finally she reached the white stone that said DAVID SEAN MCGRATH, SGT US MARINE CORPS.

She sank to her knees to the right of the headstone and thought about her brother. She talked to him for a while, about going to the alumni fund-raiser, told him about Grandpa Morgan trying to twerk at his anniversary party. She figured David would get a kick out of that.

Then she talked about Rainbow Dog. She pulled a shot glass from her bag and set it in the grass in front of her.

"This is the last one I have," she said. "I don't know if I'm going to make any more or not. I planned to, but…" Then she told him all about the fire, about lending half of the insurance money—that she was going to use for Rainbow Dog—to Justin for his half of the deductible.

"Remember how I had that crush on him way back when? Well, it's not a crush anymore. I'm full tilt in love with him. And I think part of me hoped he'd have so much fun helping me with Rainbow Dog that he'd change his mind about leaving Blue Mountain. That maybe he'd fall in love with me, too, and want to stay. But then I got all tangled up in who believes in me and who doesn't—like it really matters. Because you know what? *I* believe in me. I can make Rainbow Dog happen. You told me you liked the idea."

She frowned. "Not sure what that whole business was about telling Justin he had to come home and look out for me—"

"I think he really wanted *you* to look out for *me*, but he knew my ego wouldn't understand that."

Allie jumped up and whirled, finding Justin, leaning on a crutch.

"Why are you here?" It was probably a rude question, but unless something was terribly wrong, she didn't understand why he'd come here, where he was so determined not to be.

He held out his hand to show her the shot glass he carried. Just like the one she'd put down.

Her gaze shot to his. He shrugged and ran a hand through his hair, biceps stretching the red USMC T-shirt he wore. And then she saw it. The watch. On his wrist. He was wearing David's watch.

He saw where she was looking and lowered his arm. "Can we walk?"

They strolled, not touching, along the paved path. Then Justin spoke, stopping her in her tracks.

"Dave died because he was going to get this watch for me to wear."

Allie's sense of unreality expanded, and then she was focused on Justin, listening to every word, because she knew he'd never repeat this story.

He tugged her hand to get her moving again. "I'm not

going to be able to tell you about it if you're staring at me."

When they were walking again, he said, "This was our good-luck watch. We took turns with it." He laughed. "Actually, we made bets, and the winner got to wear it out on patrol—but basically, it alternated back and forth between us.

"The last time, we'd bet on whether—God, I don't even remember the details. Something about which new guy was going to piss off the LT first. But the outcome was in question. Anyway, I swore I won. He disagreed, but said he'd let me have it that time. We were heading out on a patrol and realized that we'd left the damned thing on my bunk. I was already all armored up and Dave wasn't, so I convinced him to run back to get it."

They'd stopped again, but he didn't seem to notice. He didn't see that she was looking at him again, because he was gazing far away and into the past.

"I was sitting there waiting, and there was an explosion. Some asshole insurgent with an RPG. As soon as it went off, I knew. Everyone else was yelling to take cover or heading out to find the fucker, but I was looking for Dave.

"And there he was. Lying there in the middle of the street, holding the goddamned watch. His legs were—" He broke off then and looked at Allie. "It was bad. But he was still alive. He was conscious, and I told him it would be okay, that we were going to take care of him, and he just shoved this fucking watch at me and said, 'Look out for Mom and Eve, and take care of Allie.'" Justin pinched at his eyes, then wiped the tears on his jeans. "I just kept telling him he was going to be fine, to shut the fuck up, but then he was just... gone."

Allie didn't know what to say. She knew the basics, of

course. The soldiers who'd come told her mother David had been killed in an attack, had died immediately of his injuries. Justin had confirmed that he'd been nearby, but that was all he'd ever said, until now.

He looked at her then, his beautiful eyes full of pain. "I'm so sorry, Allie. I'm so sorry I didn't go back for the fucking watch myself. I should have—"

"What? Died instead?"

He shrugged.

She thought for a moment about what to say. Around the lump in her throat, she said, "I miss David with every cell in my body. I'll miss him forever. But it happened. And we still have you. We don't know what would have happened if you'd gone back. Maybe he'd have gone with you. Maybe… we can spend the rest of our lives on maybe. David was not a what-if kind of guy."

At that, Justin smiled. "That's true."

When David made up his mind about something, he went for it. He didn't look back or spend time considering the options.

"I miss him, Allie. I just miss him so much."

Of course he did. They'd grown up together, gone to war together. Looking at Justin now, she realized she wasn't the only one who'd lost a brother.

"Thank you for telling me that," she said.

He nodded.

She let go of his hand and put her arms around his waist, and he, miracle of miracles, returned the embrace. As a matter of fact, he held on to her for dear life. She felt his heartbeat, strong and honorable and true, and she knew that no matter what else happened, she was not going to stop loving him.

"What changed?" she asked him. "Why did you put the watch on and come here today?"

He shrugged. "This is probably setting a bad precedent, but you were right."

She grinned. "Well, duh, but about what, specifically?"

"About not letting him go. I felt so responsible that it didn't seem fair that he had to be dead and that I could get to have peace."

"Do you? Have peace?"

He leaned over, breathed deeply. "When I'm with you, yeah."

"Really?" She pushed him away, disbelieving. "Peaceful" was the word she was least likely to use for their time together.

"Well, usually," he told her. "But what. The fuck. Do you think you're doing, selling your Blue Mountain stock?"

• • •

"I want to make sure you can go out West."

Justin's heart, which had been functioning fairly evenly, hiccuped.

"I'm not going to be a smoke jumper."

A million emotions crossed Allie's beautiful face before it settled on dismay. Not the response he was looking for. "You can't stay here," she told him.

"Why not?"

"Because you can't. I can't look at you for the rest of my life, knowing you gave up something you want to do, so that you could pay me back for a stupid accident I was as much responsible for as you. I can't have you resenting me and marrying stupid buttface Merilee, and if you'd had the money, you would have lent it to me, and not expected—"

"Shhh." He cut her off with his fingers across her lips, wishing he could dip one inside, but figuring he'd get it bitten off just now.

"I'm not going to be a smoke jumper because I want to stay at Blue Mountain and learn more about the business. And I'm not going to marry Merilee, because I was kind of hoping that *you* were my girlfriend."

"*I'm* your girlfriend?" She smiled behind his fingers, and he thought it might be safe to touch a fingertip to that lush bottom lip, which he did. She nipped it, but in a good way.

He nodded.

"And you *want* to stay at Blue Mountain? When did this happen?"

He thought for a moment. "Somewhere between the hot tub at home and the bar at the hotel in Atlanta."

"So you're going to work for your dad?"

He nodded. "At least, I will until Brandon comes back from whatever deserted island he's having his early midlife crisis on. Then, he says, he'd like me to become a corporate spy, if you'll hire me."

At this, Allie threw her arms around Justin's neck and he laid a big fat kiss on his luscious lips. "I think you're swell, Sergeant Morgan."

"You're not too bad yourself." He pulled her softness against him, hoping to be able to hold on to this feeling for the rest of his life.

"Well, I'll be damned. And this isn't part of some stupid hero-promise-debt thing about David?"

"It's got nothing more to do with Dave than the fact that if he'd have told me you had a crush on me back in the day, I'd have been more sensitive to your feelings and not acted like such a horse's ass."

She gasped, eyes widening. "You did *not* read that notebook."

"Babe, you kinda left it on the floor of the camper."

She covered her face. "I want to die of embarrassment."

"Please don't do that. I have a lot more making up with you to do."

"How far's the camper?"

Epilogue

Six weeks later

Bathroom next to the office of Rainbow Dog Liquor Company, on the first level of a farmhouse across the road from Blue Mountain Bourbon.

The knock on the door shattered Allie's paralysis, and she hurriedly shoved everything back into the plastic bag.

"Allie?" Eve called. "Are you okay? You've been in there forever. You're never gonna believe who just pulled up."

Allie unlocked the door so Eve could come in, then pulled the curtain aside to peer out at the tent that had been erected for the grand opening party. She couldn't see anyone other than Caleb and Sherry unloading snacks.

Eve slid inside, and Allie tried to drop the drugstore bag behind the shower curtain into the bathtub that doubled as a filing cabinet for business records.

"What's that?"

Damn.

Allie's hands shook as she reached back and retrieved the bag, but lifted it up when Eve reached for it. "You don't want to touch that, there's pee everywhere."

"What? Why is there—" Her eyes grew round. "Oh. My. God."

Allie dug through the bag and pulled out the damning stick with the plus sign on it.

Eve peered at it, leaned to the left and squinted, repeated the view from the right, and finally agreed. "That's positive."

Footsteps sounded outside the door.

Eve's eyes got, impossibly bigger. "Is Justin gonna freak?"

"Screw Justin, I'm freaking!"

Right on cue, another knock on the door. "Allie? Babe? You in there?"

Without waiting for an answer, the door opened, and Justin's massive self entered. Eve edged around him as he looked at both women. "Am I interrupting another weird sister ritual?"

"Nope, no, not at all. I've got to go check on...things." And Eve disappeared, like the chickenshit she was, leaving Allie and Justin alone.

"Sneezy?" The old nickname had somehow become his pet name for her. She was still babe and his girl, but no one else would ever be Sneezy.

His blue eyes searched her face, then looked down. At her hands. One of which was holding a positive pregnancy test. "Holy fuck. Are we pregnant?" His face lit up like the Fourth of July and Christmas, with trick-or-treat sprinkled on top.

He wrapped her in his arms and lifted her, peppering her

face with kisses, then setting her down, gently, and dropping to his knees.

He patted her tummy and spoke. "Hey, little tadpole person. I'm your dad, producer of the fantabulous wonder-sperm that fought through ancient spermicide-treated latex and spazzed out mom-tubes to find the egg that is making you." He pulled up her T-shirt and kissed her stomach then, blowing raspberries.

Allie giggled and shoved at his shoulders. "Stop it. You're going to scare it."

"Him. I'm pretty sure it's a him."

"Uh-huh."

He shrugged. "Just wait and see." He stood then. "So, um, I guess we officially need to be engaged now, huh?"

"We don't have to be," she said.

He just looked at her.

"Wow. You are one romantic proposer."

He dropped back to one knee and pulled some toilet paper off the roll, twisted it up, and wrapped it around her finger. "I'll do a better job when I've had a chance to find some change and get to the gum ball machine."

"I don't want anything fancy, Justin. I don't need a ring at all. I need you."

"You've got me." The sincerity in his eyes was all she needed, forever.

He cleared his throat, and she prepared herself for a romantic declaration. What she got was, "But I was sent in here to get you to come outside, because your mother's here."

• • •

Justin worked hard to keep his knees from shaking as he escorted his fiancée outside their home.

He looked back at the aged farmhouse, and what had been a ramshackle example of down-home country charm suddenly transformed into a falling-down firetrap on the verge of condemnation, now that it was the future home of his wife and children.

Shit just got real.

But Allie was shaking harder and working to hide it. He hadn't really had time to ask her how she felt about this. When that condom had broken, things had been different between them—too new, completely unsettled, so he understood her fear and reluctance about motherhood. But had that changed now that they were an official, real, long-term couple?

They'd have to deal with that later, because looming in front of them right now was Lorena McGrath, frozen fake smile in place, ready to release venom when the time was right.

"Hello, Mother." Allie smiled, her beautiful, honest smile.

Justin knew how much it meant to Allie that Lorena had shown up for their Rainbow Dog Launch Party, even if she wasn't behind the concept.

"I'm glad you could make it," Allie continued.

Her mother nodded and looked at him. "Justin."

"Hi, Mrs. McG. There's a table over there for the families, if you want to join my mom and dad. I think we're gonna say a few words and then have a toast."

As the assembled guests found seats at the tables or gathered around the edges of the tent, Caleb and Sherry passed out shots of Rainbow Dog.

"Do you know what you're going to say?" he asked Allie.

She turned to him, those hypnotic green eyes wide and

panicked. "I did. But now…I have no idea. Can you…can you do it?"

"Uh… Okay." *Shit.* He was the worst public speaker ever. Where the hell was Brandon when he needed him? Dude could at least do the Cyrano thing and remote-transmit something sensible into his ear that he could repeat.

"Thank you." She smiled up at him, her belief in his ability surrounding him and giving him superpowers.

"I love you," he murmured, taking the hand with the tissue paper ring on it and kissing it, then placing it on her belly.

Her eyes widened, and she looked sideways at the table of parents, who were, yes, looking right at them…

He cleared his throat. "Hey, everyone. Uh, thanks for being here today. We're here to celebrate the launch of Allie's business, Rainbow Dog. It was her idea from the get-go, and she worked her ass off to make it happen. Even though a lot of people told her she should do something else, this is what she wants. And as far as I'm concerned, what Allie wants, Allie gets."

There were a few snickers in the crowd.

"So, let's drink a toast to my girl Allie and her colorful imagination!"

He took a sip of liquor—this one was cherry—while Allie slugged down a glug of icy bottled water.

Someone from the crowd called out, "Whatsa matter, Allie? Sample too many flavors last night to drink a toast to your own product? Or do you know something about this drink that we don't?"

She looked at Justin, and her lips tilted, she shrugged, and said, "Might as well tell 'em."

"Well, yeah, as a matter of fact, there is something we're

not telling you, but it's not about bad whiskey," Justin said, looking toward his parents and Lorena.

His mother smiled, excited pleasure already sparking from her. How did women know these things? Lorena's faux pleasant facade had a few cracks, but he couldn't read those at all. And his dad wore a puzzled frown, probably wondering how soon he was going to lose his investment.

So Justin looked back at Allie. "You all know that I love this girl here. We were waiting until we had the business off the ground and out the door before we planned a wedding, but we've decided to move things up a little."

He held up her left hand with its twisted toilet paper engagement ring.

Everyone hooted and clapped while Allie grinned and hugged him. Her arms around his waist were the best thing he'd ever felt. Except when she did it naked.

"So yeah. We're moving things up a little, because we don't want little Davey McGrath Morgan to get here before the ink is dry on his parents' marriage certificate."

There were more noises from the crowd, but Justin didn't hear them, because he was looking at his bride-to-be.

"Allie McGrath, you have been a little part of my life as long as you've been alive, and I can't tell you how grateful I'll be if you agree to be all of my life for—"

He was suddenly aware that they weren't the only two people standing in front of the crowd. Lorena was standing next to them, hands folded in front of her, perma-smile in place.

"Mom? We're kinda in the middle of something here." Allie's eyebrows were pinched in concern. They'd all been waiting for Lorena to crack. Justin had just hoped it wouldn't happen in front of everyone they knew.

"I don't want to interrupt, but I think you need something here," she said, holding out her fist. "My mother-in-law gave this to Allie's father to give to me, and I had planned to give it to David. Since he's not here, he would have wanted you to use it instead of that ridiculous bit of bathroom tissue."

She opened her fist and revealed the enormous blue topaz ring that she'd worn forever.

Both Allie and Justin stared at it, then her.

"Mom…"

"Mrs. McG…"

"I suppose you'll have to start calling me Mother now, won't you?"

Justin looked at his own mom, who was covering her mouth, trying not to laugh, no doubt imagining Justin greeting Lorena the way he did her, with a big smooch, "Hey, Ma," and a twirly hug.

He nodded and took the ring. "Thank you, ma'am."

Lorena's smile cracked a little, something glistened in her eye, and she grazed Allie's arm with her fingers.

After his future mother-in-law glided back to her seat, Justin refocused on Allie.

"So whaddya say, Sneezy? Want to catch a cheap flight to Vegas tomorrow?"

"Don't you dare!" both his mother and Lorena shouted together.

Allie laughed and kissed him. "Maybe we should carpool to the courthouse instead."

"Only if we can get the judge to dress up like Elvis."

"Fine, but you still owe me a karaoke serenade."

Acknowledgments

So many people held my hand, kicked my butt, and yanked my arm along the road to get this story told that I'm probably going to miss a few, but here goes!

Major thanks to Nicole Resciniti, the best agent in the universe and Supreme Goddess of Great Ideas, who said, "Why don't you write about bourbon?"

Which leads me to the bourbon industry: thank you for landing in Kentucky. Everyone who has spoken to me about distilling has been amazing. I've taken a few liberties, and claim full responsibility for any mistakes—please forgive me, I'll buy the next round!

Thank you, Liz, for giving me a read and being such a positive force in my world. I love being an Entangled author!

Robin, you've been amazing to work with. Omigod, you get my jokes (well, at least you pretend to, and that's HUGE). Thank you *so* much, and I look forward to more fun and games!

To the Saturday at Skips girls and guy, thanks for being there; I miss you!

Kathryn—for all those early rounds of reading—you da bomb.

For my Monday Night Homies—especially Kim B—y'all have given me the spiritual fitness to work and not let this project derail me, one chapter at a time.

As always, thanks to my parents and my in-laws for your support.

And finally, to my three favorite kids and the best husband I've ever had, I couldn't—wouldn't—do it without you.

Wait! One more thing. Operation Homefront—the charity that Justin donated his military pay to—is a real organization, one of many groups that help our active and veteran warriors and their families, and they all need our support.

About the Author

Teri Anne Stanley can do (and has done) just about anything, especially if the directions are on the internet: turn dryer lint and old lottery tickets into paper, make posing suits for female bodybuilders—heck, give her a sheep and some cherry Kool-Aid, she'll give you a red sweater. She can also sequence your DNA or provide sex therapy for rats.

But what she'd rather do is write sassy, sexy, fun romances populated with strong, smart heroines and hunky heroes. Along with her three favorite children and a couple of dogs, she and Mr. Stanley live just outside of Sugartit, which is—honest to God—between Beaverlick and Rabbit Hash, Kentucky.

Also by Teri Anne Stanley...

DEADLY CHEMISTRY

Made in the USA
Lexington, KY
04 April 2017